"Sir Rowan, can you tell me why my poems create such a stir?"

Catherine's question was as sincere as her confusion.

"I have heard there is a hint of scandal about them," Sir Rowan said with much amusement.

"The only scandalous thing, sir, is that no one reads them. It seems to be common practice in town to form an opinion of a book based on no acquaintance whatever with its contents."

Sir Rowan could find nothing to say in defence of such an unspeakable practice. "If your poems are one jot as passionate as you are, Miss Neville, they must be well worth reading."

A flush of embarrassment and pleasure caught Catherine off-stride. "I fear you shall be sadly disappointed, sir."

Sir Rowan leaned closer to speak in confidence. "I shall be the judge of that, Miss Neville. I intend to take them to bed with me. You shall be my companion for the remainder of the night."

With a wry smile, he bowed and took his leave of her while Catherine fought to keep the ready laughter from escaping her lips.

Books by Barbara Neil

HARLEQUIN REGENCY ROMANCE
21—LESSONS FOR A LADY

Don't miss any of our special offers. Write to us at the
following address for information on our newest releases.

Harlequin Reader Service
901 Fuhrmann Blvd., P.O. Box 1397, Buffalo, NY 14240
Canadian address: P.O. Box 603,
Fort Erie, Ont. L2A 5X3

THE CELEBRATED MISS NEVILLE

BARBARA NEIL

Harlequin Books

TORONTO • NEW YORK • LONDON
AMSTERDAM • PARIS • SYDNEY • HAMBURG
STOCKHOLM • ATHENS • TOKYO • MILAN

For Marilyn

Originally published July 1990
Second edition October 1990

ISBN 0-373-31130-3

CHAPTER ONE

CATHERINE NEVILLE pulled her bonnet close to her fair face and slunk down in the carriage, but it was too late. Lord Mogglemere had spied the Perrot crest on the carriage, and he had recognized Catherine by the honey-gold curls and strong profile that no bonnet could entirely conceal.

"Oh, ho, there, Miss Neville!" he shouted from his curricle as it drew alongside the carriage.

She pretended not to hear. He continued shouting and waving, while she continued deaf.

His lordship had spotted her in front of Hatchard's and had followed her inside. She had contrived to dodge him by hiding among the bookshelves, but he had haunted the doorway, preventing her escape. A diversion in the shop caused him to turn his head momentarily, and seizing that opportunity, Catherine had run out the door and called to Dolby, the coachman. Jumping down from the box, Dolby had asked no questions. In a flash, he let down the steps, handed her inside, closed the door, and leapt to the box again, setting the horses to before the young nobleman could gather his wits. He now raced toward Curzon Street.

Putting her head out the window, Catherine implored the coachman to drive faster. As those were Dolby's favourite words in all the world, and as he was by now accustomed to admirers chasing the young lady through the streets of London, he instantly obliged. Gleefully, he urged the chestnuts toward, through and around the traffic until they had outstripped Lord Mogglemere's pretty pair. Thus he managed to get Catherine to Curzon Street before his lordship's curricle turned the corner of the square. Proudly, Dolby handed Miss Neville from the carriage, and humbly, he received her hasty but heartfelt thanks.

When the door was opened to her at Perrot House, Catherine entered hurriedly, handed the maid her pelisse and sought the safety of the sitting room. A moment later, the footman announced Lord Mogglemere.

"I've got you at last!" he cried, striding into the room. He was a tall, gentleman with a shock of red hair that confounded all attempts to iron it into a curl. "Didn't you see me wave to you?"

Catherine calmed herself by inspecting a japanned screen. "I am surprised you thought to call, sir. As I expect you will attend Lady Perrot's party tonight, I should think anything you have to say might keep until then."

"Yes, it might have done, but there is certain to be a crowd around you tonight, and I shall never contrive to get a word in."

"You have something particular to say to me?" Catherine asked with as much patience as her considerable force of will could feign.

A horrific thought suddenly overcame his lordship at this juncture, so that he enquired in an earnest whisper, "I do not disturb you, do I? I should not wish to disturb you if you are rhyming."

"I am not rhyming, my lord. I am sitting here, idly gazing out the window." Catherine sat down in the window seat and looked with fixed determination at Curzon Street.

"Ah, when an ordinary person sits gazing out the window, she may be thought to be idling," he said reverently, "but when a poet such as yourself does so, she must be thought to be composing." Here he showed his teeth in what he evidently thought was a smile. "Tell me, Miss Neville. Are you writing another book of sonnets?"

Catherine regarded him steadily. When she had first come upon the Town, she had been a shy young woman, often accused of behaving like a mouse. Celebrity had robbed her of the luxury of mousiness, however, and she had been forced to learn firmness.

"Is that what you wished to ask me?" she said. "If it is, I am afraid you have wasted your time chasing me and have lathered your horses to no purpose. I am not writing another book of sonnets. I am sorry for the one I did write."

"Oh, then you *did* see me chasing you! You have been funning me, Miss Neville!"

Catherine raised her eyes, sighed and searched her mind for a way of escaping her visitor. To her rescue came Miss Philippa Perrot, eldest daughter of the house and a young lady skilled in the extraction of wisdom from the sermons, essays and writings of the noblest sages. At present, she carried under her arm a volume of *Epistles—Elegant, Familiar, and Instructive, Selected from The Best Writers, Ancient as well as Modern, intended for the Improvement of Young Persons and the General Entertainment.*

"Lord Mogglemere!" Philippa cried, blushing fiercely. "I did not think to find you here so early. Mama's party is hours away yet. You will attend, won't you? We depend on seeing you here."

"Miss Neville and I were speaking of her poetry," he replied.

"Poetry," Philippa intoned, " 'by the certain method of allurement, leads both to learning and virtue.' "

"And it rhymes very prettily, too," his lordship added.

Catherine watched as the two seated themselves on the sofa. Slowly she inched toward the door.

Pointing at her book, Philippa informed his lordship, "I believe that somewhere here, Sir Philip Sydney states the case accurately. He says that poetry seduces its readers into doing as they ought."

"Seduces!" said the young gentleman. "I have heard certain allusions suggesting that Miss Neville's poems are not quite the thing, but I did not think they might be used for purposes of seduction. My mother is sure that a book with such a title is improper for a young lady to write, but, I confess, I see nothing out of the way, and I have examined it exhaustively for anything that might put one to the blush. The poems bounce along in a very jolly fashion, it seems to me, and I like the one about the daisies. If there was anything seductive, I wish you would point it out to me."

"What Sir Philip meant," Philippa explained, "is that moralizing rarely succeeds in reforming the generality of people. Only those of superior abilities know how to take a bald moral to heart. The others must be won over by poetry."

"Oh, that's what he meant, was it?" Lord Mogglemere said.

"Would you like to hear what else Sir Philip says?"

Catherine, knowing she could rely on Miss Perrot to keep his lordship well occupied for many minutes, was at liberty to tiptoe from the room.

A moment later she scratched on the door of Lady Perrot's chamber. Her ladyship was indisposed, and her younger daughter Daphne, who had nothing else to do, kept her company. As she reclined on a divan with a cold cloth over her brow, her ladyship bemoaned the delicacy of her constitution. Daphne, meanwhile, rummaged through her mother's jewel box, and as she tried on an assortment of earrings and hair combs, she made faces at herself in the glass.

When Catherine peeked in, Lady Perrot beckoned to her saying, "My dear child, how charming of you to visit me. I daresay I shall be sick to fainting tonight, but I shall get through the ordeal somehow."

"You are perfectly well," remarked Daphne irritably. "You have the constitution of a dray horse."

Ignoring this, her mother stretched out her hand to the visitor.

Catherine took the hand, saying, "I am very sorry you have the headache again, my lady. I do believe I have one myself."

Lady Perrot shot up. "You have the headache! No, no, you cannot be allowed to have the headache. Here, you must lie down and allow me to send Daphne for a cup of tisane."

While her ladyship stood and pushed Catherine down onto the divan, she shouted an order to Daphne, who did not move to obey but, instead, held a spray of pearls to her hair and peered in the glass to admire the effect.

"You must not take sick, Miss Neville," Lady Perrot entreated. "It would be too bad of you to miss the party."

"I'm afraid I must miss it," Catherine said. "I cannot possibly attend another party."

"We shall send for Dr. Moz. He will have you right again by this evening."

"He never seems to do you any good, Mama," Daphne observed, sampling her mother's rouge box.

"Thank you," Catherine said, "but I do not need a doctor." As she spoke, she rose purposefully from the divan. "I intend to begin packing my trunks. I shall go to visit my sister, Anne. She has been wanting me at The Priors these many weeks."

"I detest the country," Daphne declared. "There are birds everywhere. One cannot sleep past noon for the noise they make. One grows accustomed to the noises of London, but the chirping of birds is insupportable."

With decision, Catherine said, "There may be difficulties in country life, but I have imposed upon your hospitality quite long enough."

"It is not long enough at all!" her ladyship cried. "Why we have hardly begun to make use of your celebrity."

Catherine replied, "I do not see what use it can be to you, my lady. It has been nothing but vexation to me."

"Why, I intend to get husbands for my daughters out of it."

Amazed, Catherine sank down on the divan again. "How can my celebrity possibly win husbands for the Miss Perrots?"

"By bringing young men to our door. I should not be surprised if there were a young man lurking hereabouts this very minute, hoping to catch a glimpse of the famous Miss Calvinia Nutter, authoress of that charming little book of sonnets, whose name I cannot recall just at present."

"In point of fact, Lord Mogglemere is in the sitting room with Miss Perrot now," Catherine confessed.

"There, you see!" stated Lady Perrot.

Daphne danced out of her chair and hooted. "Lord Mogglemere and Philippa. It is quite perfect! The most prosing pair in all of Christendom."

"Lord Mogglemere is worth forty thousand at least," cautioned Lady Perrot. "I should not object if Philippa married forty thousand pounds."

"Well, I hope Miss Neville gets me a gentleman with curls. Lord Mogglemere may be rich, but his hair is a fright. And he is amazingly dull."

"He is not dull," the mother contradicted. "He is literary. And Miss Neville will get you no one unless you can help me persuade her not to be ill and not to desert us before the end of the season."

"My lady," Catherine said earnestly, "I have grown weary of being stared at and looked over. Everyone wants to know if I am as scandalous as the title of my book. I only disappoint them."

"Well, I daresay you would be less disappointing if you were foreign. The ton adored the Russians when they came to Town, and they trotted after that Austrian prince every day in Hyde Park. However, as a famous poet is what you are, we shall have to make do."

"I am flattered, but I must decline. I cannot endure another party."

Here Lady Perrot pulled back her shoulders, and levelling a severe look at Catherine, she said, "Have you forgotten that I took you in when you were a nobody, and I had nothing to gain by it?"

"You took her in because your brother married her sister and he paid you to do it," Daphne pointed out.

"That was ages ago. Now we are delighted to have Miss Neville purely on her own account." Then, turning to Catherine, she went on, "But if I had not taken you in, my dear, you would still be a mousy little country girl without any admirers at all."

Catherine coloured. "Perhaps I should have done better to remain as I was. That would be preferable to being admired by the likes of Lord Mogglemere."

"I can promise you, my dear, if we can marry him to Philippa, you will be protected from him forever."

"I scarcely know what to answer."

Her ladyship smiled. "Permit me to assist you then, for I feel certain you will know your duty when you realize that Philippa's future happiness depends entirely on you."

"On me?"

"Yes," Daphne interjected, "for if Philippa does not catch Lord Mogglemere, I am sure no one else will have her, and then she will die an old maid, and I shall be obliged to die of shame."

"You see," added her ladyship with satisfaction, "Daphne's future happiness depends on you as well, for she cannot catch a husband unless you are here to bring the gentlemen calling. Indeed, the happiness of the entire Perrot family rests with you, my dear, for if his lordship has the expense of these girls the remainder of his days, I am sure he will have to go to the moneylenders. As for me, well, I suffer from migraine of the head, you know, and when I fret about my dear children, I can feel my temple pound as though it were beating a tattoo."

Slowly Catherine rose and walked to the centre of the boudoir. Looking about her, she contemplated the heavy responsibilities, of which, a moment ago, she had been blissfully unaware. She considered the hospitality that

Lord and Lady Perrot had extended to her. She considered Lady Perrot's desperate hopes for her daughters. And she considered that if Philippa married Lord Mogglemere, he would be justly punished for hounding her so mercilessly through the Town.

WITH HIS IVORY horsehead walking stick, Sir Rowan Heath tapped on the roof of the carriage, signalling the coachman to stop. The conveyance immediately paused in front of an unprepossessing building on Fleet Street. The baronet emerged from the conveyance, looked about at the cold, drizzly night and entered the establishment. He took the steps easily, two at a time, then knocked with his stick three times on a badly chipped door. When no answer came, he threw open the door and went in.

There he found a chamber littered with dusty tables and scatterings of plain and printed paper. He tapped his stick on an uncluttered spot of table, waiting to be greeted. The silence informed him that sterner measures were required. Consequently, he strode into the private chamber at the end of the room, and there he found his quarry, with his arms folded on the desk and his head resting upon them in innocent sleep. After observing the sleeper for a moment, Sir Rowan poked him in the back ribs with his stick.

"I'm nearly finished! I swear it!" cried young Mr. Anthony Omsett, starting awake. Then, seeing who it was who had wakened him so unceremoniously, he complained. "I say, Heath, what are you doing here?"

"I've come to collect you," said Sir Rowan. He picked up a paper that lay under the young man's elbow and read it.

"Give that here!" Tony cried, attempting—unsuccessfully—to snatch it away. When he saw that he was not going to retrieve the paper, he sighed, asking without enthusiasm, "You've come to collect me for what?"

Handing him the paper, Sir Rowan smiled. "How can you write such drivel, my friend? You must take your oath, Tony, that henceforth you will write at least one intelligible page a day. As to why I am here, it is to collect you for Lady Perrot's party. You recall my telling you of it."

Yawning, Tony replied, "I recall your saying the idea of it infused you with the most lively sense of ennui. I recollect it because I thought it a rather interesting turn of phrase."

"If you knew Lord and Lady Perrot and their frog-faced daughters, you would know that I was merely being accurate."

"Why do you insist on going where you know you will be bored?"

"I have promised Lady Perrot to bring a literary light with me this evening."

"What literary light?"

"You, my dear fellow. You are one of the scribblers who signs his name to this charming little review. Hence, you are a literary light. Besides, Byron is engaged, and I have no one else ready to hand."

"Do you really think I am a literary light?"

"Hardly, but you will oblige me, Tony, by behaving like one tonight. Her ladyship wishes you to meet a literary light of her own, and I have pledged that you will engage the authoress in conversation for a full fifteen minutes. I have also promised that you will make at least four brilliant statements that will be quoted in the *Times*."

"I'm afraid it's impossible. I have work to do."

"Don't be silly. You cannot call this work."

Mr. Omsett rose, adjusted his coat and his dignity and said a little loftily, "If you do not think it is work, then I should like to see you do it."

"I should be only too happy to do it, only we are engaged this evening. Come, let's be off."

"It really is impossible. I have a book of sonnets to review, a book I have not finished reading as yet and I have a new book of essays to dissect in print. I shall be at it all night, I'm afraid."

"And I am afraid that you must put it off until the morrow."

"I cannot put it off because we must go to press tomorrow. There lacks only these two pieces, and I have promised Mr. Wolley that the review will not be late. In his turn, he has promised to keep me on if I do not disappoint him again this month."

The baronet tapped his stick against his gloved hand, then looked about him to make certain no one else was able to overhear. Coming close to Tony, he said, "Do you know what is at stake here, old fellow?"

Surprised but curious, Tony confessed that he did not.

"Lord Perrot's port. Have you never heard of it?"

"I can't say I have because I haven't. I haven't even heard of Lord Perrot."

"Well, he is not much in himself, but he has a store of port that is reputed to be extraordinary. I mean to have a taste of it."

"I see. You wish to go to Perrot House tonight because his lordship will serve port to his guests."

"Of course not. Lord Perrot serves his guests vinegar masquerading as champagne. But I am told by his brother-in-law, Binky Reardon, that he keeps a decanter of his port in a small room not far from the drawing room."

"Binky Reardon? Do you mean the Earl of Tice-hurst?"

"Yes, are you acquainted with old Binky? He is a thickheaded fellow, but he does know port. Look here, I have a map, drawn by Binky himself."

Tony licked his dry lips and peered at the map Sir Rowan had taken from his pocket. "It is very tempting and all that, Heath, but I have these reviews to get out."

"Very well, I shall assist you. With the two of us working, we shall be out of here and into Perrot's port within the hour."

"You cannot write a review."

"Of course I can. Any simpleton can."

"What have you ever written that was not in the political line?"

"I am certain I wrote something at Oxford. Lord knows I was there long enough, and I expect my tutor would have insisted upon my putting pen to paper once or twice."

"What did you write at Oxford?"

"Let me think. As I recall, I wrote a treatise on swans. Yes, that was it. I believe I documented the fact that the creatures are monogamous. Very odd fellows, are they not?"

"Swans! You never wrote about anything so ridiculous. You are quizzing me."

"See here. What is so mysterious about writing a review? It cannot be so different from writing a political essay."

"Even if it were precisely the same," Tony said, "I should be sceptical, for you never wrote a word without first dipping your pen in poison. I should not be surprised if Percival called you out or if one of your other victims hired ruffians to waylay you on the street. It would not be the first time.''

Sir Rowan smiled. "You flatter me, dear boy. Now let me see that book of poems you spoke of.''

Tony handed him the slim volume, saying, "You are too careless, you know. One of these days, you will reap what you have sown.''

The baronet turned to the book's title page and smiled. Slapping an elegant gloved hand on it, he declared, "Why, nothing could be easier. What we have here is a book of sonnets by a lady. Everyone knows what a book of sonnets by a lady is. One has only to fill in the blank spaces and one has a review ready to hand.''

"But it will take time to read the thing, Heath.''

"Such books are not meant to be read. They are not meant to be reviewed either, but we have not the time to argue aesthetics just now. I shall write this review, and I shall finish in such good time that I shall be able to assist you in writing the other.''

"I suppose I do not absolutely mind your reviewing the poems,'' Tony said, wavering, "for, in spite of your style, I admire the taste and intelligence of your essays.''

Speaking in a warning voice, and raising his stick for emphasis, Sir Roman said, "You must never allude to my having taste and intelligence. A man of my position has enough trouble maintaining his reputation as a simple, ordinary fellow without his friends undermining it.''

"You are too rich and have terrorized too many members of Parliament with your essays to be deemed either simple or ordinary.''

Sir Rowan said with distaste, "If you must laud my reputation as an essayist, do so behind my back. And please do not speak of my riches, I beg you. We must devote ourselves at all times to getting money and laying it up, but we are never to speak of it. Otherwise, we shall be taken for Americans."

"See here, Heath. I do not mind your quizzing me, but you ought to read the book if you are going to review it. I saw one or two poems that struck me as rather fine."

"I shall review this little book of poems without reading a single word, just to show you how it may be done. It will be the most astounding review your obscure little publication has ever had the privilege to publish."

Mr. Omsett sighed and attempted to retrieve the volume. "Perhaps I had better do it myself."

"No. You may sign your name to it, but I shall write it. I quite look forward to it, in fact. Now let me see. What have we here? Ah, yes. *A Pilgrim's Passion* by Miss Calvinia Nutter. Good God! Can there truly be such a creature as Calvinia Nutter? What can her father have been thinking of, to saddle his daughter with such an appellation?"

Tony shuddered. "You will not be too harsh, will you, Heath?"

Sir Rowan sat down at the desk, swept it clean with his stick, then set a piece of blank paper before him. "How shall I begin?" he mused. Setting the stick aside, he picked up a pen. "Ah, I can taste the port even now. I only regret that it will wash away the pleasing taste of venom."

CHAPTER TWO

LADY PERROT'S DRAWING ROOM was spacious and airy. Its high decorated ceiling dripped chandeliers which bathed the animated faces of her guests in soft candlelight. Brocaded chairs and settees were arranged in clusters. In the centre of the room, a large, round ottomanlike sofa invited guests to sit and converse as intimately as they liked. But the guests ignored the clusters and the ottoman. They preferred to stand where they could catch a glimpse of one of the celebrated guests Lady Perrot had promised to provide.

In one part of the room a group of about twenty gathered around Miss Calvinia Nutter, who stood by a light satinwood card table without any hope of being allowed to sit down to whist. She wore a puff-sleeved, soft blue gown ruffed at the hemline and ribboned under the bosom in pale lavender. The bone fan she carried was painted with violets. Her hair was swept up in back with combs, and fair curls wisped along her forehead. Lord Mogglemere stood in rapt attention, waiting for a word from the poetess, cherishing it when it came. Nowhere did Catherine see Miss Philippa Perrot or any other prospect of rescue.

Sir Rowan Heath and Anthony Omsett arrived well after midnight. The baronet greeted his hostess with apologies, explaining, "Tony was obliged to scribble tonight. These literary fellows are mighty serious, are they not?''

Lady Perrot took pity on the serious young man. It was too bad of him to be constrained to toil these past hours when he might have been furthering his acquaintance with her youngest daughter. Taking him in tow, and promising him an eventual introduction to a bona fide poetess, she went in quest of Daphne.

Sir Rowan then greeted his host, Lord Perrot, who grimaced upon hearing himself addressed.

"What are you doing here?" his lordship enquired, putting his glass to his eye to inspect the baronet.

"Her ladyship was so kind as to invite me," said Sir Rowan cordially. He relished Lord Perrot's brusqueness.

"But you never go anywhere," his lordship muttered.

"Yes, but I felt a sudden fit of sociability overtake me. You do not object to my coming?"

Lord Perrot shrugged. "As long as you are here, I suppose you are welcome."

"That is most hospitable. Lord Reardon informs me that you keep a good store of port."

At this allusion, his lordship lowered his voice and looked suspiciously about him. "Not so loud, if you please."

"Is it possible to sample it, my lord? I promise to reciprocate with a sample of my snuff. Wilson at Sharrow Mills makes it up for me."

"Alas," Lord Perrot lamented, "the port is all drunk up. There's not a drop of it left. Otherwise, I should be glad to let you sample it."

Sir Rowan smiled, having been warned that his lordship would not scruple to lie in order to avoid offering his guest a taste of the port. With a bow to his host, the baronet moved to greet Miss Philippa Perrot, who stood alone, accompanied only by *Elegant Extracts*. A moment later, undetected by the crowd, he slipped from the drawing room into the corridor.

Removing the map from his pocket, he ascertained his bearings and walked to a room at the far end of the corridor. It was a small room, and cold, not inviting enough to be often frequented by members of the household. On a carved table by a sofa stood a decanter and a number of glasses. From the ruby shine of the decanter, Sir Rowan surmised that it housed the precious brew.

He had poured out a glass and was just about to sip when the door opened and a young lady dressed in blue crept in backward. Apparently, she saw something frightening in the corridor, for she started back, closed the door quickly and sighed. As she turned around slowly, her eyes fell on Sir Rowan. She had to clap her hand to her mouth to stifle a cry.

A voice in the corridor shouted, "Miss Neville! Where have you gone to, Miss Neville? I vow, I shall find you out."

"You are Miss Neville, I collect," said Sir Rowan, gesturing toward her with his glass of port.

"He must not find me," Catherine said. There was a plea in her voice.

As he watched her lean back against the door, her breath coming quickly, her face turned so that she might listen for sounds in the corridor, Sir Rowan forgot momentarily about the port. "He's coming," she whispered. "I hear his footsteps. What shall I do? Where may I hide?"

They looked about the room for a screen or a drape behind which a fugitive might conceal herself, but nothing came to hand.

"He will come inside any moment!" Catherine cried.

"Here," said Sir Rowan, setting down his glass untasted. Taking her by the hand, he drew her to the sofa and bade her sit down. When she complied, he sat close beside her. The door opened, and, at the sound, he pulled her to him and kissed her.

"Why, Miss Neville!" Lord Mogglemere exclaimed at the sight of the poetess in the arms of a gentleman.

As Miss Neville's lips were occupied, she vouchsafed no answer.

It occurred to his lordship that this might not be an auspicious moment to question Miss Neville on her preference for the Italian sonnet over the Shakespearean. He therefore announced, "I shall speak with you another time," and withdrew.

As soon as the door closed, Catherine pushed Sir Rowan from her. Fire was in her eyes as she slapped his face.

"And that is my reward for coming to your aid!" the gentleman declared in a martyred tone. He rose, walked to his glass on the table and soothed himself with a sip of it.

"How dare you!" Catherine said.

"How dare *I*? How dare *you*!" he retorted. "I placed myself in the utmost peril in order to assist you, and this is how I am repaid."

"What peril?" she demanded.

"Well, for one thing, I expect Mogglemere will call me out. We shall meet at Green Park at dawn. Green Park is so fashionable, you know. Mogglemere will want to meet where the ton prefer to meet. I shall be killed for my trouble without so much as a thank you from the lady I saved."

"Lord Mogglemere does not strike me as the duelling sort."

"Yes, that is true. And I should find the ordeal rather exhausting myself. But even if I am not to get shot, there is a worse peril. Mogglemere will set it about all over Town that I was seen kissing a lady at Perrot House. My reputation will be ruined."

Catherine could not help laughing. "I suppose I shall be forced to marry you to preserve your good name."

He smiled back. "There, that's better. Now, I shall pour you out a glass of this splendid port."

Catherine rose and peered at the decanter. "That is Lord Perrot's port."

"I know."

"He never lets anyone drink it."

"I know. Have some."

Handing her a glass, he instructed, "You must not take too much and you must sip it slowly, or your head will be filled with goose feathers in the morning."

Catherine knew she ought to return to the drawing room. Prudence and propriety required it. However, certain that Lord Mogglemere would pounce upon her the instant she entered, she could not bring herself to go back just at present. Instead, she studied the dark-haired gentleman who stood before her. He wore a coat of soft grey with blue breeches, a waistcoat of ivory and a simple white linen cravat. His figure was well proportioned, and although his stature was medium, he appeared taller, owing to his imposing air. He carried his glass to the sofa and sat. Then he invited her to do likewise.

Unable to suppress her curiosity about the gentleman who had blithely kissed her, then helped himself to Lord Perrot's port, she accepted the invitation. Sitting down, she said, "I daresay you think my hiding in this room very odd."

"Not at all. The gentleman admires you, and you hate the very sight of him. Nothing could be clearer."

"I do not see what right Lord Mogglemere has to torment me in such a manner. If he were not a nobleman, I should say he was very ill-bred."

"The nobility are known for their ill-breeding. It is the foremost privilege of rank."

"But he persists in chasing me through highways and hallways. It is provoking in the extreme."

"Well, you are a very pretty young woman. I daresay he cannot help himself. If I were given to chasing, I should chase you through highways and hallways myself."

"Pretty!" Catherine said scornfully. "Pretty, you call me. Why when I first came upon the Town, I was declared to be not at all the thing. Too fair. Not fair enough. Too rosy. Not rosy enough. Too yielding. Not yielding enough. Now, suddenly, I am become a goddess!"

"A goddess. I say, that's coming it a bit strong."

Her ire roused now, she did not hear her companion's irony. She stood up and paced. The baronet watched as her blue-clad figure marched up and down before him.

"They promised faithfully to engage him to Philippa. He was not to plague me ever again. And this is the upshot of my appearing tonight. I am persecuted!"

Sir Rowan sat back, admiring the glow in her eyes and the passion in her gestures and countenance. Sipping his port, he did not know when he had been so well entertained at Perrot House.

"I am surrounded to such a degree that I am not permitted to breathe. My footsteps are dogged whenever I go out. I am pursued to the farthest reaches of this house. And then I am unceremoniously kissed by a stranger."

"See here, young lady, you may rail all you like against Mogglemere and the others, but you are not to speak of the matter of our kiss in the same breath."

"And why am I not?" Her expression challenged him irresistibly.

"Because the kiss meant nothing. It was merely a ruse to rid us of your pursuer."

This statement stopped Catherine. She took a breath and her eyes opened wide. "It meant nothing?"

"Precisely. I was not kissing you. I was saving you. I felt it as a duty, no more."

"Oh."

"I might as well have been kissing that statue." Here he swept a hand in the direction of a pedestal, on which sat the bust of a dead Roman.

"Is that all it was?"

"Exactly. Your lips were no more to me than that cold marble which frowns at us even now."

"Cold marble?"

"Do I detect a note of doubt?" he enquired. "For if you do not believe me, I shall be glad to kiss you again and prove that what I say is no less than the truth." He rose from the sofa as if to indicate his readiness to perform the demonstration.

Suspecting that he was quizzing her, Catherine glanced at him, and found him looking at her so starkly that she could not meet his eyes. "I believe you are laughing at me," she said.

"I laugh at everybody, especially myself."

"Why?"

"I am a careless fellow, who finds that there are only a very few things in this world worth stewing over. The rest deserve to be laughed at."

"Are you advising me to laugh at Lord Mogglemere?"

"It would save you a good deal of running through hallways and highways."

"And what of gentlemen's kisses? Should I laugh at them as well?"

"No."

Shyly, Catherine regarded him. "What do you advise there?"

"Return them."

He came a step nearer to her then, and she wondered if he would kiss her again, but he only bowed and held out his arm so that he might escort her back to the drawing room.

THEY HAD NO SOONER RETURNED than Catherine was once more swallowed up in a throng of admirers. As Tony Omsett was engrossed in conversation with the younger Miss Perrot, and as the port had already been tasted and approved, Sir Rowan had no reason to linger at Perrot House. Nevertheless, he sought out Miss Philippa Perrot, who sat by herself in a corner.

"Tell me," said the baronet after exchanging inconsequential conversation with the young woman, "are you acquainted with Miss Neville?"

Pleased at the baronet's attention, Philippa replied, "We have been on the most intimate terms for more than a year, and in that time, I have conceived the greatest compassion for that pitiful creature."

Sir Rowan regarded her with interest. "I cannot imagine why you should feel sorry for her. She seems a very handsome young lady, and she is certainly very much sought after."

Philippa shook her head sorrowfully. "As the Bard says, 'The purest treasure mortal times afford is spotless reputation.' I am afraid Miss Neville's reputation is dreadfully spotted, and her loss must be irrecoverable."

"You do not approve of her being so much admired?"

Philippa replied thoughtfully, "Her situation serves to teach me a valuable lesson, and where there is good to be derived from an evil, it cannot any longer be regarded as an evil. I should like to expound on that valuable lesson, if you please."

Before Sir Rowan could reply, Philippa continued, "I have learned, you see, that one risks blame and notoriety when one permits the free and unfettered expression of a gift. I myself have the gift of extraction. That is to say, I am able to scout out bits of wisdom in my extensive reading and to repeat them in the course of ordinary conversation. You no doubt noticed that I quoted Shakespeare just now. That is the sort of thing I do excellently well. I had some notion once of collecting my extracts in a journal, but Miss Neville's example teaches me never to set a word to paper."

"You show great sagacity in refraining from writing," said Sir Rowan gravely, "and even greater sagacity in recognizing that others live their lives principally in order that we may learn valuable lessons."

Blushing at this high praise, Philippa bowed her head, then raised her eyes to the baronet's face. To her disappointment, she found him looking in the direction of the group gathered about Miss Neville.

"You alluded a moment ago to a gift," said Sir Rowan. "What gift is it that has caused Miss Neville to be so sought after?"

"You do not know?" Philippa exclaimed.

"Know what?"

"She has written a book of poems."

"Good Lord, another poet. I had thought better of her than that."

"Her book is the talk of London. You must have seen it."

"I am careful not to see anything of that kind."

"*A Pilgrim's Passion*, it is called."

The baronet exhaled, closed his eyes, then opened them. "*A Pilgrim's Passion*," he repeated grimly.

"Yes. She had intended it to be called *A Pilgrim's Passage*, but apparently there was a mistake in the printing."

"What you say is impossible. *A Pilgrim's Passion*—or *Passage*, or whatever the deuce it is titled—is the work of a nervous female who calls herself Calvinia Nutter."

Philippa tittered at this description of the authoress. "How very droll you are, Sir Rowan. But Miss Neville and Miss Nutter are one and the same. 'Calvinia' for Catherine and 'Nutter' for Neville. Clever, is it not? I assisted her in devising the nom de plume."

Sir Rowan did not reply. He watched Miss Neville edge her way gracefully out of the group that had hemmed her in. He saw Lady Perrot swoop down and capture her. He saw her ladyship lead the young woman to a settee. Then he saw her introduced to Mr. Anthony Omsett, literary light and noted reviewer.

AN INTRODUCTION between Sir Rowan and Miss Neville took place some time later. Neither betrayed any hint that they had met previously, and when they were left alone, he bowed and she nodded graciously. The gentleman expressed his delight at meeting a renowned poet. The lady expressed her readiness to reveal his unlawful port drinking to Lord Perrot if he said another word about her poetry.

"You wish me to keep mum on the subject," he said. "But why? Your poems are bruited everywhere."

"Sir Rowan, you are a man of the world. Can you tell me why my poor poems should create such a stir?"

"I have heard that there is a hint of scandal about them."

"The publisher attached that scandalous title. I had nothing to do with it. But I assure you, the poems themselves are completely innocent."

Looking into her blue eyes, he could well believe in the innocence of her poems. "Londoners are fond of celebrity-watching," he said. "They like to follow noted personages about the city, even going so far as to snatch off pieces of their clothing to treasure."

"If Lord Mogglemere so much as touches my hem, I shall scratch his eyes out."

"Hearing you say that with such spirit, Miss Neville, I am determined to read your poems."

"No one reads them, sir. They borrow the book from one another but do not trouble themselves to read it."

"Do you mean they presume to make much of you without first reading your poems?"

"Yes, it is despicable. But it seems to be a common practice in Town to form an opinion of a book based on no acquaintance whatever with its contents."

Sir Rowan could find nothing to say in defence of such an unspeakable practice. "If your poems are one jot as passionate as you are, Miss Neville, they must be well worth reading."

"Oh, let us not talk of them. Can you not find another subject?"

Casting about him, Sir Rowan at last bethought himself of swans.

"Swans?" Catherine exclaimed. "I know nothing about swans."

"Whereas I know a great deal about them, heaven help me," Sir Rowan replied.

"Well then, swans it shall be." Clearing her throat, she said, "I have observed that the swan is a beautiful, graceful creature. There. I believe that will serve for a turn of the conversation."

"As regards swans, Miss Neville, you must look beneath appearances. If I may presume to advise so illustrious a personage as yourself, I must point out that to see only the creature's beauty is to do an injustice to his estimable character. The swan is, without equal, the noblest species of waterfowl or of any other species."

"What? Nobler than the Englishman?"

"Far nobler. The swan, you see, is famous for fidelity to his mate. When did you last hear of an Englishman blessed with such a character?"

"Is it only the male swan who boasts of such uncommon virtue?" she asked. "What of Mrs. Swan?"

"Therein lies the true superiority of the species, for the lady returns her husband's regard in equal measure and will remain faithful until he leaves her a widow. If one wishes to find fidelity anywhere, one must look to the swans."

Catherine regarded him closely. "You are ironic, sir, which I take to mean that you are cynical. I conclude someone has broken your heart."

"I am cynical, it's true. That is why no one has ever broken my heart. And what of your heart, Miss Neville? Methinks the heart of a poet must be oft cracked in twain."

"I am not cynical, as you are, but my heart remains whole. You will think me insensible, I fear, and will not wish to read my poems after all."

"By no means. I intend to take them to bed with me. You shall be my companion for the remainder of the night." On that daunting announcement, he took his leave, and soon after bidding his host and hostess good-night, he quitted the house.

THE FOLLOWING DAY, Sir Rowan visited Tony Omsett in the chambers of *The Gentleman's Review*. Bleary-eyed and fuzzy-headed from the previous night's gaiety, Tony moved among the dusty tables and the drones who worked at them with an air of preoccupation. Sir Rowan followed him.

"Look here, Tony," said the baronet, "I've changed my mind about that piece I wrote last night."

"Changed your mind? Whatever do you mean?"

"I wish to withdraw it."

Tony stood still, turned and stared at his friend. "You importuned me to be allowed to write it. You insisted!"

"Perverse of me, I own," Sir Rowan confessed. "I don't know what I was thinking of."

"Well, it's too late."

"Nonsense. You can replace it with another review."

"I do not have another review."

"I mean to give you another."

"Another review of the same book of poems?"

"Yes. This review will please you, for I have actually read the book this time."

"Did you like it?" Tony enquired, inspecting an illustration handed to him by a clerk.

"I liked furthering my acquaintance with the authoress."

"I saw you engage her in conversation last night. I do not know how you had the face to look her in the eye."

"To tell you the truth, old fellow, I regret the matter of the review altogether. I ought never to have pressed you. I am sorry I did, sorrier than I imagined I could ever be."

"As well you ought to be," Tony said, approving the illustration and sending the clerk on his way.

"Will you retrieve that piece from the printer and substitute this?" asked Sir Rowan, handing the young man a paper.

Taking it, Tony smiled at his friend archly. "We are not suddenly developing scruples, are we, Heath?"

"Certainly not. We are merely trying to keep out of hot water with a charming young lady."

"You like her, do you?"

"I find her interesting," Sir Rowan declared.

"In the same way you found that actress interesting when you were nineteen and hid in her boudoir for a fortnight."

The baronet smiled. "You must confess that she *was* an interesting lady. As I recall, she found me interesting as well. But enough of my misspent youth. You must go and get that review and tear it to pieces. Now!"

Laughing, Tony said, "Very well. I shall see to it." Thereupon, he rolled up the new review, and as he marched off with it, he used it to scratch a well-formed ear.

CHAPTER THREE

THE YOUNG LADIES gathered the following afternoon in Catherine's bedchamber to assess the previous night's gala. Daphne declared that Mr. Anthony Omsett's hair curled charmingly, and the gentleman might have proved as charming as his coiffure, if he had paid more attention to her and fretted less over *The Gentleman's Review*. Mr. Wolley, the publisher, had recently established Mr. Omsett as editor, and the young man had confided to her that he meant to devote all his time and energies to making his mark in the world of letters. For her part, Daphne meant to see what she could do to distract him from his purpose.

Philippa was not as pleased with Lord Mogglemere as she had anticipated. It seemed the gentleman could not sit still long enough to hear her quotations but must always be dangling after Miss Neville or Mr. Omsett. In contrast, Sir Rowan Heath had struck her as a remarkably sensible man. He had sat next to her for some length of time, listening to her opinions with more than polite interest, and he had even praised her sagacity.

Catherine added little to these opinions. She had found Mr. Omsett pleasant enough. But when he had spoken to her of his journal, she had found her attention wandering. Seeing Sir Rowan seated in a corner with Miss Perrot, she had wondered what subject engrossed them in such lively conversation.

In Sir Rowan, she had found rather a contradiction. His words were frequently satiric, and she suspected it would be wise to be on guard against his caustic tongue. Nothing, it appeared, gave him pause or ruffled his aplomb. At the same time, she had sensed a strength of conviction and feeling beneath his insouciance. She had found him penetrating, interesting and amusing. Catherine did not know when she had met a gentleman who made her feel so uneasy and yet so curious to know more of him.

As to Lord Mogglemere, she resolved at the very next opportunity to speak to him seriously. If she was going to resign herself to remaining in Town until the summer, she really must do something about his relentless assiduities.

THE THREE GENTLEMEN left their cards for the ladies that same day, and on the next, they each paid a morning call. Later in the week, it chanced that they all called at the same time. First to arrive was Lord Mogglemere, who thought perhaps, as it was such a pleasant spring day, that Miss Neville would like to ride out with him. As it happened, Miss Neville did not like to ride out with him. She could not abide a pleasant spring day, she assured him.

When Sir Rowan and Mr. Omsett appeared, they too suggested an outing, one that included all the young ladies. Lord Mogglemere quickly informed the newcomers, "Miss Neville does not wish to ride out. The weather does not suit her."

"It is dreadfully sunny and balmy today," Sir Rowan observed. "I cannot blame Miss Neville for wishing to stay indoors."

Mortified, Catherine said, "If the rest of the party likes to go out, I shall not demur."

"Oh, no!" Lord Mogglemere insisted. "We cannot have you sacrificing your comfort for ours. You would not wish to risk disobliging your muse."

Desolately, Catherine looked from Lord Mogglemere's freckled face to Sir Rowan's fine-featured one. She found the baronet smiling at her.

"Not long ago, Miss Neville expressed an uncommon interest in swans," Sir Rowan said. "Perhaps she would put aside her abhorrence of the weather in order to view one or two examples of the species."

"Out of the question," Mogglemere cried. "And if Miss Neville does not like to go outside, I am sure I do not."

"If it is to see the swans," Catherine said, "I should be happy to go."

Sir Rowan bowed at this politeness, but his lordship declared, "You only say that out of regard for our comfort. I put it to you, what sort of comfort are we to enjoy when it is won at the expense of your own?"

Sir Rowan stepped in to say, "Naturally, I should never think of asking Miss Neville to sacrifice two hours of her time simply in order to stroll through the park to view the waterfowl. I make the invitation in the interest of poetry, for I am certain Miss Neville will be inspired to write a sonnet on the swan. So you see, we have a high purpose to justify this excursion. No one will dare to accuse us of merely taking our pleasure in the park."

Catherine could not help smiling at Sir Rowan's persuasions.

Lord Mogglemere decided that Sir Rowan's argument might have considerable justice. "After all," he reasoned, "a poet must go out and view nature now and again if she is to write about it."

Philippa nodded. "Pope says that all nature is art," which piece of philosophy his lordship did not hear, for he noisily clapped his hands and declared that he should be pleased to allow Miss Neville to ride out.

It was now a matter of concern to find a site fit for the viewing of swans. As it was not Sunday, Sir Rowan said, he and his companions would not be admitted in Kensington Gardens. Perhaps it was just as well, for the gardens had fallen into a disgraceful state of decay; even the charming orangery had been allowed to suffer. The fault might be laid at the King's door, for it was well known that his preference for Buckingham had permitted Kensington's neglect.

"Then you must not look for swans in Kensington," declared Lady Perrot, who foresaw that the outing would give her daughters time with the young gentlemen that might be turned to profit. "You must go to Hyde Park."

"The Serpentine is an artfully conceived lake," Sir Rowan allowed, "and might do very well, except that the walk through Hyde Park is generally too congested to afford ease and pleasure, let alone the opportunity for flights of poetic imagination."

"Perhaps we ought not to think of viewing the swans," said Philippa. "Perhaps ducks will do as well."

"Ducks!" exclaimed Lord Mogglemere in disgust. "There is nothing either elegant or poetical in a duck," he declared, an observation that prompted Philippa to shrink into her chair.

"Now, Green Park is a garden strongly favoured by the fashionable set of late," said Sir Rowan, "but as our object is to see rather than be seen, I do not consider that Green Park will answer our purpose."

While the discussion proceeded, Catherine observed the baronet. His air was ironic, amused. His dark blue coat and velvet collar set off his dark hair. As he stood in the centre of the parlor, he was perfectly aware that every eye was on him and that his listeners would instinctively follow his lead. He took their deference as his due, and if he once or twice could not resist laughing at it, he also could not resist meeting Catherine's eyes to see if she laughed with him. That she did laugh appeared to give him pleasure.

"Indeed," Sir Rowan stated, "there is only one park in London suitable for the viewing of swans, and that is St. James's."

"Good Lord," whispered Mr. Omsett in his ear. "You really do know something about swans, don't you?"

"I certainly hope so," Sir Rowan returned in a low voice.

To St. James's they would have set forth on the spot, but Miss Philippa Perrot rose from her chair and with her face as pale as death said, "Although the sights and sounds of nature never fail to inspirit me, I am forced to decline to view them at this time. I beg you will all excuse me." Tragically, she moved to the door.

Her sister prevented her from making an exit by saying irritably, "Do not be so vexing, Philippa. We are not going to view nature. We are going to view the swans."

Turning to the company, Philippa put a hand to her bosom and declared, "Of all the creatures under heaven, there is none I abhor so much as the swan."

Her mother protested, "I am sure if Lord Mogglemere and Sir Rowan approve the swans, they must be very good ton and you ought to like them."

"They are vile, odious beasts," Philippa replied.

Approaching her, Sir Rowan enquired gently, "Miss Perrot, have you perchance quarrelled with a swan? I know they are capable of being quarrelsome fellows, despite their beauty."

Philippa regarded him with gratitude. "A swan tried to kill me once."

The others looked amazed at this revelation.

"My sister is right," Daphne put in. "I recollect that nasty bird very well, and I shall never forget the look in its eye. It *did* mean to kill Philippa. No doubt she was quoting at it."

Lady Perrot, who had no intention of permitting her daughter to let slip a chance to walk out with Lord Mogglemere, went to Philippa, took her hand, and said, "My dear, do you not know any proverb that touches on the evils of bearing a grudge?"

"No," Philippa answered with unwonted brevity.

"But there must be one in those books you read?"

"I can't recall any, Mama."

"Will you agree that if there is no such bit of philosophy, there ought to be?"

"Yes, but what has this to do with the swan who wished to kill me?"

"Only this, that with the assistance of your friends, you will learn the virtue of forgiveness. You will overcome your aversion to the creatures so far as to throw them a few crumbs. I shall ask cook to supply you with crumbs." Here she summoned her footman and sent him below stairs with instructions to return with crumbs.

Philippa swallowed and darted her eyes about in search of an escape.

At this juncture, Catherine stood and interceded, saying, "We ought not to press Miss Perrot if she does not like to go. Indeed, she would no doubt find our talk of swans tiresome."

"Fiddle!" said Daphne. "There is nothing Philippa likes so well as tiresome talk."

"I have a particular motive for insisting that Philippa accompany you to see the swans," her ladyship said. "I am hoping that if she goes to St. James's, you may teach her not to be afraid." On this last phrase, she looked directly at Lord Mogglemere.

"She has every reason to be afraid," said Sir Rowan. "A mute swan will attack anybody who dares to trespass on what he imagines to be his territory. Miss Neville is correct in saying that Miss Perrot ought not to be pressed."

Philippa shot her mother a look of triumph.

"What swan would dare attack my poor daughter if you, my lord, were there to protect her, and you, Sir Rowan?"

Lord Mogglemere protested, "Madam, my presence only guarantees that I shall be attacked, too!"

Lady Perrot would have despaired of success had not Sir Rowan come to her rescue. "Very well. As you have your heart set on it, my lady, I shall personally see to Miss Perrot's safety." He made a gallant bow and offered the young lady his arm. "Will you do me the honour of permitting me to act as your protector against all manner of swans and suchlike creatures?"

Catherine saw the frightened Miss Perrot raise thankful eyes to the baronet's. Then Philippa took his arm and walked out with him. The others followed. To Lord Mogglemere's great joy, he found himself escorting Miss Neville.

As THEY DROVE in Lord Mogglemere's carriage, which held six comfortably, Sir Rowan soothed Miss Perrot's fluttered nerves by unfolding the history of the park's unequalled collection of waterfowl. In days of old, he said, the marshy lands of the park had been populated by duck and birds of all kinds. Charles II, either despite his habits of debauchery or because of them, was an avid naturalist and took a fond interest in winged creatures. He improved their waterways through the park, which resulted in a vast increase in their numbers. Charles was often seen taking the air in St. James's to feed his pelicans, storks, geese and swans.

The baronet's manner of delivering this lecture was amusing enough to entertain the entire party, but Catherine soon found her attention fixed on his most enchanted listener, Miss Philippa Perrot. Indeed, that young lady was so fascinated by Sir Rowan's fund of bird lore that she did not utter so much as an epigram during the entire drive. Catherine found herself uneasy on this account, for not only did Philippa fail to vouchsafe a word to Lord Mogglemere, but his lordship failed to vouchsafe a look at anyone but Miss Neville.

The party entered at the gate and made at once for the lake. A glimpse at Miss Perrot informed Catherine that the young woman was no longer hearing anything Sir Rowan said and that the closer they drew to the water, the paler and more wide-eyed did she grow.

"I believe Miss Perrot is frightened," Catherine said to their escort.

Pausing, Sir Rowan said to Philippa, "You need not walk down to the water if you do not like it."

"Oh, but I must," Philippa whispered. "Mama will fly out at me if I do not. And she wishes me to feed the swans these crumbs." Here she held up a small sack tied with a ribbon.

"Ah, yes, she has her heart set on your befriending the fellows. But your mama is not here now and need not know it if you choose to sit upon that delightful rustic bench under the sycamore."

Taking Philippa's elbow, he led her to the bench, and there they arranged themselves. Miss Perrot exhaled a breath of relief, and from this safe distance, she and her protector watched their companions amble to the lakeshore.

Daphne proclaimed herself too energetic a walker to stand gawking at the water. She persuaded Mr. Omsett to take the course around the lake, and the two were soon lost to view behind a stand of shrubs.

Lord Mogglemere and Catherine stood at the lake's edge, looking for swans but seeing no sign of them anywhere. For some time, they stood in silence, watching the water ripple under the breeze. Catherine saw in the distance the towers of the palace framed by budding trees.

"Do you not wish to seize this moment," asked his lordship, "to compose a verse?"

Catherine turned to look at Miss Perrot and Sir Rowan on the bench. "A verse on what subject, my lord—the paucity of waterfowl?"

He tittered. "Your wit is so amazingly lively. But you must tell me what your eyes see as you view this picturesque scene. All I see, I'm afraid, are trees and water."

"But that is all I see."

"Oh, I am sure you see the feelings and thoughts they evoke as well."

Still observing the two on the bench, Catherine said, "My lord, you flatter me. Indeed, you make a great deal too much of what you are pleased to regard as my poetic sensibility. Please believe I am an ordinary woman, like Miss Perrot."

Now he, too, looked at the seated couple. "You are not the least bit ordinary, and certainly not like Miss Perrot!"

"I should think you and Miss Perrot ought to have a great deal to say to each other," Catherine said, "for you are both of a literary turn of mind."

His freckled face went blank a moment while he contemplated this pronouncement. "Miss Perrot would be very well, I daresay," he declared at last, "if I had never experienced the delight of your company. Now I am spoilt for others, I fear."

This was the opening Catherine had sought. She fixed him with a stern look and wagged a finger at him, "You must stop this nonsensical talk, my lord. You must stop chasing me through streets, shops and houses. It is not kind of you."

His eyes went wide. "But I admire you."

"You must stop that, too."

He sighed. "What else is there for me to do? I have no useful occupation. Therefore, I look to assist you in your poetical endeavours."

"If you truly wish to assist me, you may keep Miss Perrot company while Sir Rowan locates a swan for me to look at."

"Will that please you?"

"Inexpressibly."

"Then I shall say no more, but go at once, and if in so doing, I may in some small way foster the gift of creation with which you have been endowed, I shall be most humbly grateful, for I worship at the feet of greatness, even when it is found in womankind."

Catherine remained tranquil enough to say, "You have my permission to leave now."

A moment later, he was seated by Miss Perrot, and Sir Rowan joined Catherine by the lake.

"It seems we have come on a fool's errand," he said. "After all my encomiums on St. James's, the place has the ingratitude to produce not a single bird for us to admire."

"It is just as well, I expect," Catherine said, "for you have been occupied with Miss Perrot all this time."

He gave her a quick glance. "But you were so well entertained by his lordship. I am sure you cannot have felt neglected."

"We are here to speak of swans," she said, "not of me and Lord Mogglemere. Surely we can find one or two specimens."

He pointed to a mound of water plants and told her, "That is a swan's nest, I believe. The mama and papa are sure to be home shortly."

"A nest?" Catherine repeated. "I should never have guessed." She stared in its direction, but the baronet detained her by grasping her firmly by the arm. "We shall stay here, if you please," he said. "The nest most likely belongs to mute swans, which means they cannot chase us away merely by shouting at us at the top of their lungs. They must resort to violent means to protect their cygnets."

Catherine's eyes fell on his hand, which still held her arm. Then she looked into his brown eyes. Recalled to decorum, he removed his hand and stepped away.

Lightly, she observed, "I believe you said that the swan represents everything that is noble. At the same time, you say that he is disposed to be violent. His behaviour toward Miss Perrot has certainly been anything but noble.

You overrate him, I think. He sounds very much a bully to me."

He smiled. "But a noble bully, for who would remember to be polite in defence of one's home and hearth?"

Catherine could not help asking, "Sir Rowan, why on earth did you take up the study of swans?"

"To find a subject sufficiently inconsequential as to disoblige my family, who were expecting great things of me. I might have married to disoblige them, to be sure, but that would have inconvenienced me even more than it did them."

"Why did you wish to disoblige your family?"

"That is what young people do, is it not? I say, Miss Neville, I thought we were poking after swans here, but you appear to be poking after me."

Catherine coloured. "Look," she cried all at once. "There are the swans. They are swimming our way. We had best give up our ground before they attack us."

"Those yellow-and-black-billed creatures are Bewick swans, not mute swans and they are not likely to attack us. They are more likely to cut us altogether. Except at feeding time, they do not appear to think well of the generality of human creatures."

"I have the impression, Sir Rowan, that you do not always think well of the generality of human creatures, either."

He met her direct look. "Yes, but I begin to like them better and better," he said.

Just then, Miss Perrot came up and stood between Catherine and the baronet.

"You are feeling better?" he enquired.

"The contemplation of nature is not as uplifting as one supposes, especially when one is bored to distraction," Philippa answered with a pout.

"It cannot be that you prefer the company of swans to that of Lord Mogglemere!" said Sir Rowan.

Philippa blushed. "I do not mind the company of swans, now that you have undertaken to protect me. In such a circumstance, I am sure I shall not come to any harm."

Catherine, who would have preferred to see Miss Perrot stay where she was, turned to glare at the swans. There were now six or seven of them swimming toward the shore and honking loudly.

At the sound, Philippa grasped the baronet's arm.

"They will not attack you," he assured her. "In fact, this might be an auspicious time for you to feed them some crumbs."

Nervously, she untied the ribbon and emptied the contents of the sack at her feet. The sight of food brought the birds waddling onto the grass. As they gathered about her boots, Philippa froze. One fat fellow marched up to her and honked at her in a scolding tone. She started and whimpered and flailed her arms at him in an effort to drive him off. Her movements frightened the fellow. His companions were startled as well and began to flap their wings and squawk more noisily.

In response, Philippa screamed, which sent the swans into flight, skimming low over the water, then back over her head.

When Catherine next looked, she found Miss Perrot collapsed in the arms of Sir Rowan. Lord Mogglemere, who had witnessed the entire scene from the bench, now came running toward them, shouting for help.

"Quiet!" Sir Rowan snapped. "Do you wish to mortify the young lady by causing everyone to stare at her?" Carefully, he lowered her onto the lawn. He removed his fine blue coat and folded it into a cushion. Then, kneeling by Philippa's side, he gently raised her head and slipped the coat under it. After removing Miss Perrot's glove, he felt for her pulse. It appeared to Catherine that his touch was amazingly tender for so languid a gentleman, and that Philippa had done herself a world of good by contriving to faint.

CHAPTER FOUR

MR. OMSETT AND DAPHNE returned to find Miss Perrot lying unconscious on the grass. Sir Rowan would not permit them to come close to her. "She requires air," he explained. "If she is allowed to breathe freely, she will wake that much sooner."

"Should we not do something?" demanded Lord Mogglemere.

"Perhaps you carry hartshorn on your person," the baronet answered curtly. "Saving that, a vinaigrette would serve."

His lordship frowned. "I wish I had thought to bring hartshorn, but it never occurred to me. I do not carry it with me, as a rule."

"Few gentlemen do carry hartshorn, as a rule," Catherine said. "Sir Rowan was quizzing you."

"I see. Well then, it is too bad I did not carry a vinaigrette. But perhaps I might fetch a doctor."

"By the time you have brought him, Miss Perrot will have recovered," said the baronet.

"Should I fetch some water?" asked his lordship. "I will be happy to use my hat, if such a measure is called for."

"If you are thirsty, Mogglemere, by all means go and fill your hat. As to Miss Perrot, she does not require a dousing, and I daresay she will not like to wake up and find herself soaked to the skin."

Taking a handkerchief from her reticule, Catherine went to the lake, stooped to wet it and wring it out and then brought it to where Philippa lay. She would have applied the cool linen to the young woman's brow, but Sir Rowan took it from her and performed the duty himself.

"I say, Heath," Mr. Omsett put in, "how do you know so much about fainting ladies? Did you study them at Oxford, too?"

Sir Rowan did not reply, nor did he appear amused at this sally. He regarded Miss Perrot with dead seriousness as he knelt beside her and held Miss Neville's handkerchief to her forehead.

Daphne tiptoed near to Catherine to say in her ear, "I think my mama was quite right to make Philippa come today. The upshot is that she has made herself the centre of attention."

Catherine asked in a low voice, "Do you mean to imply that Miss Perrot has not really fainted but is only pretending?"

Shaking her head sadly, Daphne answered, "Alas, no. My sister's talents are all in the bookish line. She has not the facility for fainting, as I myself do. I expect she really is quite unconscious, poor thing, but the calamity serves a purpose nonetheless. Look at Sir Rowan. He is nearly overcome with worry, I think."

It occurred to Catherine that Sir Rowan had now encountered one of those few events he had mentioned that were worth stewing over. His expression was grave, and he did not search out her eyes as he had done earlier.

"He is much handsomer than Lord Mogglemere," Daphne whispered. "I never thought to say this about my sister, but she has done well for herself this day."

Just then Philippa rubbed her eyes and asked, "Why am I lying on the lawn? Are we having a picnic?"

Sir Rowan removed the handkerchief from her brow and said softly, "You fainted." To prevent her from rising, he placed a restraining hand on hers.

She looked at him with glowing wonder.

"You must rise slowly. Permit me to help you," Sir Rowan said, supporting her with his strength. Mr. Omsett took Philippa's other arm to help her up.

"It is possible you may experience a little unsteadiness for a time," the baronet said. "It will soon pass, however."

Catherine said to Sir Rowan, "Miss Perrot is not the first woman to faint in your presence, I collect. You appear to know a great deal about such matters."

When he turned to meet her gaze, she saw that he was not disposed either to banter or to converse. The satiric light in his eyes had vanished. "I have had a little experience in that line" was all he said. Then he proffered his arm to Philippa, who acquiesced eagerly. The two walked toward the gate, with Daphne and Mr. Omsett following close behind.

Catherine retrieved her wet handkerchief, which Sir Rowan had let fall onto the grass, and accompanied by his lordship, she moved after the others. She could hardly keep from staring ahead at Miss Perrot and Sir Rowan. That Lord Mogglemere suffered from the same predilection became evident to her when he said, "I do not see why Sir Rowan should be permitted to assist Miss Perrot. To be sure, I was just as worried about her as he was."

There was some comfort to be derived from the sound of his lordship's jealousy, but it was swiftly overshadowed by the sight of Philippa leaning heavily on Sir Rowan's arm.

LADY PERROT COULD NOT express her gratitude enough. Sir Rowan's gallantry in saving her daughter's life must be rewarded. He must come to Perrot House the very next week to dine and sit down to cards.

"I did not save your daughter's life," the baronet said. "Indeed, if I had been the protector I had set myself up as, she never would have been so frightened as to faint. I blame myself, Lady Perrot."

Lord Mogglemere interjected, "I'm sure I should have been gallant in saving Miss Perrot's life, too, if the opportunity had presented itself. But I did offer to fill my hat with water."

Lady Perrot thanked the young lord with all her heart. She beamed as she glanced from one gentleman to the other. "You must both come and take potluck with us Wednesday next," she cried and invited Daphne and Miss Neville to add their entreaties to hers. "We hardly know how to be grateful enough," she continued. "Perhaps Perrot will offer you some of his port."

Hearing his port mentioned, Lord Perrot started. "I fear it is all gone, my dear," he said anxiously.

"Nonsense. There is a decanter of it in that small, cold sitting room that no one ever sits in." She rang for the servant who went to fetch the port.

When the wine was served out, emptying the decanter, her ladyship called for Lord Perrot to propose a toast to swans and to all manner of flora and fauna, of which she was excessively fond. Soon after, Lord Perrot murmured his farewells and set out for his club, where a man might be permitted to have a little peace without everyone plaguing him and drinking his port.

Sir Rowan reminded her ladyship that while they were enjoying the excellent wine, her elder daughter was in her bedchamber, enduring the doctor's scrutiny, and no doubt, still very much atremble. He expressed a wish to hear what the doctor concluded. On that hint, Lady Perrot dashed to Philippa.

Mr. Omsett then took his leave. His departure inspired Daphne to yawn, declare herself bored beyond bearing, and make her exit as well.

Lord Mogglemere, finding himself dissatisfied with the events of the afternoon and not at all pleased with Sir Rowan's assiduities to Miss Perrot, stayed as long as he could endure the silence, which was not long. At last, he persuaded himself to make his adieux to Miss Neville, whose muse, he hoped, had not been unduly alarmed at St. James's. On Sir Rowan, he bestowed the coldest of nods before he left.

Catherine felt that she ought to retire as well, but she did not move to go. Instead, she watched the baronet wear a path in the carpet. He did not appear to be conscious of her presence, and therefore Catherine kept very still, lest making a sound should interrupt his preoccupation.

Stopping at last, he fixed his eyes on her and said, "You blame me. I see it in your expression."

Colouring, Catherine answered, "You are mistaken. I do not think it was your fault that Miss Perrot fainted. I do not blame you in the least."

He came closer to her chair. "This is not the first time I have been responsible for such a mishap." His tone was bitter.

Catherine's curiosity was roused. For some time, she had longed to know more of the man. She wondered if he was on the point of confiding in her.

"Years ago, I accompanied my sister on a ride which ought never to have taken place. She was a fragile child, delicate of constitution from birth, certainly too ill to sit on a horse. I gave in to her entreaties, however, thinking that no harm could possibly come to her as long as I was there to protect her."

"But there was an accident, she fainted and you blamed yourself."

He drew a chair next to hers and sat. "Yes. She was ill for a very long time."

"Did she recover?"

After a pause, he replied, "No."

"I am very sorry, but still, you ought not to blame yourself."

"My sister ought to have been married and busy with her bairns, her chickens and her strawberries. It is my fault that she is not alive to enjoy these pleasures."

"You say she was of a delicate nature from birth. Perhaps her mishap had less to do with her fate than her constitution. I think you ought not to be so hard on yourself."

"Miss Neville, you know me to be a man who takes the world as it comes. I make it a rule not to stew over the tangles that drive the rest of mankind into frenzies. As a result, I am occasionally a careless—perhaps even a callous—fellow. It would not be such a bad thing, except that nearly always my carelessness ends by hurting someone else. If I bore the consequences myself, I should not mind, but I do not see that innocent parties ought to suffer."

"Miss Perrot is not your sister, nor has she suffered as dreadfully as you think. And even if she has suffered, I believe your many kind attentions to her have more than compensated."

"You do not believe any such thing. If you did, you would not have scowled at me through the entire afternoon."

"I did not scowl!"

"You did. Your disapproval was evident to me every minute. When I did not see it, I felt it."

"If I scowled—and I am not admitting to anything so absurd—it is only because you promised to show me swans, and I had barely an opportunity of glimpsing any."

He sat back, not a little surprised. "You were disappointed on account of the swans?"

Pointedly ignoring the doubtful expression he wore, she said with some asperity, "Just when you were telling me the most interesting facts about them, Miss Perrot interrupted us. We were forced to quit St. James's soon after that."

He studied her so intently that she evaded his eyes. "Am I to understand that you were unhappy merely because we were forced to leave the park early?" he enquired.

In a light tone, she replied, "I was not unhappy, but you certainly cannot expect me to compose a sonnet based on such incomplete observation as I was able to make this afternoon."

"I never expected you to write a sonnet at all. That was merely a pretext, as you well know."

She replied sharply, "Yes, a pretext for walking with Miss Perrot in the park!"

Slowly, Sir Rowan stood up and resumed pacing the carpet. This time, however, he did not dwell on his responsibility for poor Miss Perrot's grave mishap. What caught him was Miss Neville's evident tone of displeasure. Whenever he had heard such a tone in a woman's voice—and he had heard it more than a few times—it betokened jealousy. Was it possible that Miss Neville was jealous, that she resented his attentions to Miss Perrot?

He could scarcely credit it. The young woman appeared cool, wholly in command of herself, not at all likely to be subject to fits of jealousy. Yet there was that in her voice, a slight quiver of emotion, which brought him to think that she must be jealous.

The possibility ought to have amused him. Such happenstances had always amused him in the past. In the case of Miss Neville, though, he was more disposed to be careful than amused, for if she were not jealous, he would be profoundly disappointed. Turning to face her, he said, "My suggestion that we observe the swans was a pretext for walking in the park with *you*, as you may recall."

His forthrightness caused her to blush. She regretted her earlier sharpness. If she did not exercise more caution, she warned herself, the gentleman might misinterpret her tone as pique, or worse, as ill temper. Not for the world would she have him think she was ill-tempered or in any way less amiable than the adoring Miss Perrot. She wished to reply, but when the words did not come, she blushed again.

Her speechlessness moved him, and he came quickly to the rescue. Taking his chair once more, he leaned forward and enquired, "Who are you, Miss Neville? That is to say, who besides a celebrated authoress? Surely you have not always lived with Lord and Lady Perrot. Where are your family?"

Grateful for the change of subject, Catherine replied, "My father was an admiral in the Royal Navy. He was killed at Trafalgar. My mother did not outlive him by very many years."

He was all grave attention. "You have no family, then?"

"I have a sister, Anne. She was recently married to the Earl of Ticehurst."

"My good friend Binky has carried off your sister, has he?"

"Yes, he has. He also prevailed upon his sister, Lady Perrot, to offer me an invitation to stay in Curzon Street. Her ladyship was so kind as to oblige."

"Will you stay in Curzon Street long?"

"I suppose I shall, but I should much prefer the quiet of The Priors and the company of Anne to the noise of London. I was born in Hampshire and am in reality a simple country girl."

Smiling, he replied, "There is nothing simple about you. You observe a great deal, not without a satiric eye, and you do not say above a third of what you think."

"We are much alike, then," she said.

"Yes, I think we are. We have a great many interests in common, not the least of which is our curiosity about the swan."

"I hadn't the least curiosity about your precious Mr. Swan, until you puffed up his attractions, making him out to be a very model of English virtue."

He smiled. "It occurs to me that it would have been better if the swans had come at *you* instead of Miss Perrot."

At this, she snapped a glance at him. "I suppose you think I would not have fainted, as the delicate Miss Perrot did? No doubt you think me too insensible to faint."

Hearing the note of jealousy in her tone again, he replied soothingly, "I do not think you insensible at all. But if you had not fainted, I should have had the pleasure of rhapsodizing with you over the swans for the rest of the afternoon."

"And if I had fainted?"

"In that even, I should have had the pleasure of catching you in my arms."

Catherine coloured. She had never quite caught the knack of badinage as it was practiced in Town, and she did not know how to answer in kind. She answered plainly, saying, "You deny that I am a simple country girl, but I assure you, in the matter of flirtation, that is precisely what I am. I beg you, sir, do not quiz me."

He would have denied the charge of flirting had not Lady Perrot slipped into the room then and cried, "She is quite well, my dear Sir Rowan. I know it will put your mind at rest to hear that she will recover. She speaks of you continually, of your kindness and gallantry, and only wishes she were well enough to thank you in person."

"Thank me for what, Lady Perrot? For taking her where she had no wish to go, and then subjecting her to precisely what she feared? I do not merit her thanks, nor yours."

"Fiddle!" Her ladyship laughed. "My daughter is not angry with you. On the contrary, I have never seen Philippa so much in charity with any one as she is with you. Therefore, you have no choice but to allow us to thank you, and I will hear no more of your protests. He is very wrong to blame himself, is he not, Miss Neville?"

Catherine nodded. "I feel certain," she said, "that Miss Perrot does not regret her encounter with the swans, not a whit."

"There, you see," Lady Perrot said. "Miss Neville agrees, and she is excessively wise, for what is the use of a poet if she does not supply us with wisdom? Now, sir, you will come again tomorrow and the next day, and if the doctor will not permit you to visit my daughter, then you shall visit me."

He looked at Catherine when he replied, "As you insist, my lady, I should like very much to visit."

Politely, Catherine inclined her head. She then saw him take his leave, anticipating his return on the morrow.

IF CATHERINE ALSO ANTICIPATED a continuation of her recent conversation with the baronet, his next visit disappointed. The instant he entered Perrot House, her ladyship pounced upon him and brought him to a large, light parlour where Philippa had been charmingly arranged on a sofa and a fire had been lit. Through the whole of his visit, he sat close to the sofa and spoke in low tones to the patient. Their soft accents excluded the others in the room—Lady Perrot, who sat at her work by the fire, and Catherine, who sat at a table sorting dried flowers for a posy. From time to time, her ladyship glanced at her daughter and the handsome rescuer and sighed in satisfaction. From time to time, Catherine, too, glanced at Miss Perrot and the baronet. Her feelings, however, were not so contented as her ladyship's. Sir Rowan gave Philippa his undivided attention, and if he did glance up to observe Catherine at her flowers, she had no inkling of it.

After an interminable time spent in this manner, Catherine saw Lady Perrot set her work aside and excuse herself. The lady had no sooner quitted the room than she poked her head in the door again and beckoned to Catherine. "Come, my dear," she said with urgency, "I would have a word with you."

When Catherine came to her, her ladyship closed the door and whispered, "We may as well leave them to themselves for a bit. I warrant they have much to say to each other."

This hint caused Catherine to wish to return to the parlour at once, but she could not do so as long as her ladyship continued with her. Soon, however, Lady Perrot took herself off to the saloon. At that juncture, Catherine turned to enter the parlour and was surprised to find the door already open. Sir Rowan stood before her, framed by slender oaken columns, regarding her. Catherine was mortified to be discovered lurking in the hall, as though to waylay him just as soon as he should come out, but the baronet smiled and, as he closed the door behind him, observed, "I am relieved to see that Miss Perrot is none the worse for her fright. And I am glad that you are still here and have not gone out."

"I expect Miss Perrot was grateful for your visit. She admires you greatly."

He turned to face her, and came so close that she stepped back. To her chagrin, she backed against the wainscoting, so that she was stopped at the wall. She feared Sir Rowan would come closer, but he did not. Instead, he put a hand on the wall, just by her cheek, and said, "As I've told you before, I am a careless fellow. I fear I have been so careless as to forget my manners, Miss Neville. I never properly apologized to you for that kiss. As I recollect, it took place in this very house, in a room off this very corridor. You must think me remiss."

Catherine closed her eyes slightly, then opened them to return his gaze with full force. "An apology would be superfluous, I think. You told me the kiss meant nothing, less than nothing. One is not obliged to apologize for nothing."

"Good God. Did I really say it was nothing?" He raised his free hand and rested it on the wall near her other cheek. She could feel his sleeve graze her hair. He moved an inch closer.

Swallowing, she replied, "Yes, you did say it, and I am sure you cannot be so careless as to say what you do not mean."

One of his hands slid from the wall to her chin, which he held so that he might kiss her, and as she raised her lips to him, Lord and Lady Perrot were heard entering the hall. Sir Rowan was obliged to step away and attempt to appear tranquil, while Catherine endeavoured to greet her host and hostess with a smile.

As soon as they spied the baronet, Lord and Lady Perrot insisted upon accompanying him to the door and waving him farewell. They did not notice Catherine, who still stood with her back against the wall, her breath coming quickly, but Sir Rowan turned as he was led off, and his parting look gave her every hope that he would return the next day to repeat his visit of charity to poor Miss Perrot.

A little giddy, Catherine returned to the parlour. On seeing her enter, Philippa cried, "Oh, is he not the most amiable of gentlemen? Who was it who said that an excellent manner betokens an excellent character? Gracious me. I cannot recall. Nor do I care who said it. What matters is that Sir Rowan's air and manner speak of what he is. How pretty of him to apologize for the hideous swans. He will blame himself, no matter how much I protest. And his apologies are affecting, I must confess."

As Catherine returned to her posy at the table, she was forced to agree that Sir Rowan's apologies were indeed affecting.

Lord and Lady Perrot entered the parlour then, and the mother and daughter discussed the sterling qualities of Sir Rowan Heath, from his gleaming Hessians to his immaculate white cravat, from his dark coat to his cleverly curled dark hair, from his excellent figure and noble nose to his gallant air and his income of twelve thousand a year.

"I hope you do not mean Philippa to fall in love with him," said Lord Perrot to his lady. "It will not do, you know."

"Fiddle," Lady Perrot scoffed. "It will do very nicely, especially if Lord Mogglemere does not pay his addresses."

Lord Perrot shook his head ominously. "Sir Rowan appears to be a catch, I own, but he is, in reality, a dangerous sort."

Philippa sat up straight on the sofa. "Is he, Papa? How is he dangerous?" She appeared more intrigued than alarmed.

"Why, he tends to Whiggery."

"Never!" cried her ladyship. "How can you say so? He is a baronet. His lands are vast. His family are positively mossy with age. Why should he wish to guillotine his acquaintances and steal their estates?"

"My dear, he is a Whig, not a Jacobin."

"It is all the same thing—they all wish to chop off our heads and make a shambles of polite Society. It is what they did in France, and what they mean to do here."

"Sir Rowan is not a revolutionary, my dear. He is a Whig, like the Prince. But if our entire government is to turn Whig, I am sure I do not know what will become of us."

"Oh, well, if the Prince is Whiggish, I do not see what is wrong in Sir Rowan's being so. I'm sure Whiggery is all the crack, if the Prince likes it."

Philippa's eyes shone. "How do you know Sir Rowan's views, Papa? Has he confided them to you?"

"Everyone knows his political views, daughter. He publishes them in this review and that, in pamphlets and broadsheets and newspapers. His satires are everywhere, attacking the prime minister, saying that one must trade with the Americans regardless of principle and similar nonsense. I'm afraid he is a careless fellow, Sir Rowan is, and he will suffer for it."

Catherine, who had listened to this exchange with fascination, could not forbear asking, "How will he suffer?"

"He will be attacked on the street one of these nights. You will read of it in the newspaper, I've no doubt. Some minister or other will hire himself a blackguard to do the work, and Sir Rowan's corpse will be found in the morning, lying in a pothole or a puddle, pecked at by crows. Mark my words."

Philippa put her hands to her mouth. "Oh, he will be killed! How horrible. You must warn him, Papa."

"I shall do no such thing. He knows very well the risks of Whiggery. He has already been attacked twice, though it came to nothing, for he knocked the teeth out of one of the fellows and bloodied the other from top to toe. No, no, nothing I said would deter him from his infernal scribbling."

Downcast, Philippa said, "Oh, it would be too bad of him to get himself killed."

To which Lady Perrot added, "You must tell him so, my dear. And if your charming expression of concern should end in his making a declaration, why so be it."

Lord Perrot stood up and raised his eyes and his hands to heaven. Then, addressing his wife and daughter, he said, "I have told you why you must give over any idea of attaching Sir Rowan, and you have not heard a word I've spoken. You must be two of the silliest women in

Britain to think of snaring the fellow, regardless of his principles. It seems to me that the only sensible female in this room is Miss Neville. She is not so easily taken in by such a fellow. She is not likely to ignore such warnings as I've given you this day."

Here they all looked at Catherine, who blushed to think how little she deserved the compliment.

CHAPTER FIVE

IN THE COURSE of the following week, Miss Perrot felt so much recovered as to consider attending Lady Tristram's ball. With the season nearing its end, her mother persuaded her, one must look to amuse oneself as studiously as possible before being banished to the country, and as private balls were so much more select and elegant than public ones, Lady Tristram's ball must not be missed. Ordinarily Philippa consented to attend such galas only because Society exacted the duty from her. "Man is a social animal, I suppose," she had been used to saying with a shudder of distaste. But to this magnificent occasion she eagerly looked forward. It was not long before Catherine discovered the reason for her unwonted complaisance. Sir Rowan had, it seemed, let slip the fact that he meant to make an appearance at the ball, and when Philippa had made known her excessive delight at the news, he had been obliged to obtain her consent for the first set.

Lord Mogglemere arrived in Curzon Street to announce his intention of refusing his invitation to the ball. "You will, of course, be unable to attend, Miss Neville, and therefore, I feel disposed to decline the invitation as well."

Astonished, Catherine asked, "And why do you conclude that I will be unable to attend? I hope you do not think I cannot dance a reel."

"I am sure you know how to dance a reel to perfection," he said. "I only thought that your poetry prevented you from partaking of the frivolous pleasures. I expect you are in the throes of another volume of sonnets."

Catherine frowned. She had not written a sonnet or even a line of a sonnet since she had met Sir Rowan Heath. Vexed at the thought, she searched hastily for a reply. "Oh, but I am fond of dancing. If I do not dance every dance at Lady Tristram's ball, I shall be desolate. I shall certainly fall into a decline and that will put a period to my sonneteering altogether."

She had no sooner pronounced these joking words than she was sorry, for Lord Mogglemere took them as a hint to procure her promise for the first set. Politeness obliged her to accept the invitation, which, far from satisfying the gentleman, only encouraged him to ask for another. Fortunately, when he asked for a third, she was able to scold him gently and remind him that a third dance was certain to look particular and cause remark.

Lord Mogglemere was bold enough to state, "Let it cause remark. Let tongues wag, if they please. And if they do not wag in vain, I shall count myself the most fortunate of men!" On this exclamation, he levelled a look at Catherine that was evidently intended to signify adoration.

She remained adamant in refusing, however, and the gentleman at last turned his attention to Miss Perrot.

"You are looking very well," he said to her, not masking his surprise

"Yes, I am very well," Philippa assured him. She sat in a dainty cnair and, instead of carrying a volume of *Elegant Extracts*, she held a copy of what Catherine strongly suspected was a novel.

"I did not think you would look so rosy, not after fainting dead away as you did and frightening us out of our wits." His lordship seemed almost disappointed that the young lady was not absolutely prostrate.

"Sir Rowan's quick thinking prevented me from suffering anything worse," she said.

"Quick thinking, was it? Why, all he did was forbid us to do anything for you. He merely let you lie there in the grass until you woke of your own accord."

"He put his handkerchief to my forehead, which was most pleasant."

Sullenly, Lord Mogglemere looked at Catherine. "It was Miss Neville's handkerchief. Sir Rowan took it from her."

"I expect he wished to apply it with his very own hands," Philippa responded. Then she let forth a sigh and opened her book, but to Catherine's mind, she could not have comprehended much of what she read, for she did not turn the page once during the remainder of his lordship's visit.

WHEN THE EVENING of the ball arrived, Philippa appeared very much to advantage in a pale yellow muslin that clung to her large frame and exposed a great deal of shoulder and bosom. Daphne gasped at the sight of her sister decked out in a gown that was not an absolute fright. "You look nearly fashionable!" she exclaimed. "Now, if you will remember to say not a word the entire evening, I daresay the baronet will offer for you."

"Philippa has taken her oath not to say a word," Lady Perrot declared. "Everything is to go off beautifully. I have arranged it all."

Lord Perrot was astonished to see his plain daughter with her locks twisted and worked into a Grecian pile of curls. Moreover, he was not a little shocked to see that she had dispensed with her customary heavy silk to clothe herself as thinly as Daphne. "Will she not freeze?" he asked his wife. "She has been very ill lately. I am sure she will take a chill in that gown, if it may be called a gown."

Philippa smiled at this tribute and allowed her mother to fluff her sleeves and smooth her gloves.

"She is very well," said Lady Perrot to her husband. "She will become warm soon enough when she dances. In the meantime, a little freezing will not kill her."

At the first opportunity, Catherine added her quiet compliments to the noise of the family. Philippa received the sincere words with a becoming blush, and Catherine could not help marvelling at the change that had been wrought in the prosing Miss Perrot. Although the young lady's figure was too angular to be elegant and her movements too nervous to be gracious, still she struck Catherine as sparkling. It occurred to her that love might be the cause of this transformation. Miss Perrot's tendre for Sir Rowan surely lay at the bottom of it. And if Catherine had not hoped that the gentleman's affections were already placed elsewhere, she would have concluded that Philippa was in danger of becoming Lady Heath.

LADY TRISTRAM'S BALLROOM consisted of a high-ceilinged hall ringed with balconies on three sides. On one, the musicians played. On the other two, ladies walked on gentlemen's arms, fanning themselves, glancing at the crowds below and waving to their acquaintance. More than a few couples were seized with an inspiration to avail themselves of the privacy of one of the rooms off the balconies.

On the floor, the dancers awaited the call to the first set, and at that moment Lord and Lady Perrot were announced with the three young ladies. Daphne was the first to come forward. She looked round anxiously for Mr. Omsett and pouted when she did not see him. Next came Catherine, dressed in a white jaconet threaded in the bodice with wisps of gold. Her blond hair was adorned with a ring of white beads, and on her neck she wore a brooch which hung from a white velvet ribbon.

Sir Rowan no sooner spotted her than he made his way through the crowd to greet her. She saw him approach and smiled to see the marked admiration in his eyes. He clicked his heels and bowed over her hand, then stopped. As his eyes fell on Philippa, he could not disguise his surprise.

"Miss Perrot," he said slowly. "Whatever ill effects your late mishap may have had on you have now, I see, completely vanished. Please accept my congratulations."

Simpering, Philippa opened her mouth to reply, but a judicious poke in the back from her mother, whose fan was ornamented with stiff points at the edge, caused her to clap it shut again without uttering a sound.

Sir Rowan put out his arm, Philippa placed her hand upon it, and Catherine watched them move toward the line of dancers now forming on the floor. The baronet seemed to have forgotten about her presence—nay, her very existence—and Lord Mogglemere's appearance at her side to claim her for the set did little to console her.

His lordship proved an athletic dancer, given to leaps in the air and sweeps of the arm over his head. With mortification, Catherine saw that the onlookers hanging from the balcony pointed at her partner and openly snickered. The other dancers also looked her way, until it seemed to Catherine that she would have done better to stay at home that night to scribble a sonnet.

She had not spent above half an hour in Lady Tristram's ballroom before concluding that rarely had she endured so dreary an evening. Of course she had known that Sir Rowan was promised for the first dance, and of course she had known that the dance was to be danced with Miss Perrot. She had not, however, expected him to like it or to perform his bows and steps just a few yards from her without glancing longingly her way every few minutes.

When Catherine caught herself thinking these irritable thoughts, she grew alarmed. It was not like her to evince such restlessness. In general she was a calm, thoughtful, unhurried young woman, given to repressing any flutters of emotion that might ruffle her tranquillity, given to very few such flutters to begin with.

Since making Sir Rowan's acquaintance in Lord Perrot's cold sitting room, however, she had known a good deal of fluttering. The hideous thought crossed her mind that she was as idiotically in love as poor besotted Philippa, but whereas *l'amour* had metamorphosed Miss Perrot into an animated, radiant spirit, she herself was succumbing quickly to the crotchets. Her only excuse for such behaviour was that instead of dancing with the baronet as she wished, she was occupied with protecting her feet and her dress from the enthusiastic Lord Mogglemere.

It struck Catherine that she would in all likelihood feel a good deal less restless if she had been accustomed to the ways of London. She had grown up in Hampshire, and in county society she had acted very much as an observer. Known to be shy among strangers, she was permitted to sit in the corner and watch the goings and comings of others. Soon she contrived to become as much a part of the background as the chairs and portraits that lined the assembly rooms. There was one young man who had noticed her and who had managed to win from her more than a few sentences, but his father had arranged for him to marry an heiress, and so the few sentences languished, never to become a conversation.

When she had passed her twentieth birthday, Catherine grew so bold as to venture more often into the thick of activity, but always she retreated to her corner again, to observe the absurdities of her neighbours and to compose poems in her head. She was now nearly twenty-two. Unexpected celebrity had thrust her into the limelight, where she had shifted about uneasily for some time now. Some aspects of fame she had grown accustomed to: those admirers who would not dream of buying her book but thought nothing of asking her to supply them with a copy, those who sought her out at card parties to tell her what they did not like in her poems and those who wished to tell her of their own poetical flights of fancy so that she might translate them into words. But other things she could not get used to. One of them was dancing with an unsatisfactory partner who rattled on about her muse while hopping up and down and slicing the air with his hands.

The music ceased. Lord Mogglemere continued dancing until she tapped his arm with her fan. Bewildered, he looked about him and said, "What a pity they've stopped playing. I nearly had that step." He began to entreat her to let him procure her a glass of wine, when he was soundly slapped on the back and cheerfully accosted by a dark, handsome young man, very fine, and very naughty looking.

The stranger did not take his eyes from Catherine, but appraised her up and down with heavy-lidded appreciation. "Mogglemere, my dear fellow, where the deuce have you been keeping yourself? I never see you at a mill any more."

"I don't go to mills any more," his lordship replied. He did not like the way the gentleman regarded Miss Neville and attempted to lead her away.

Catherine, amused at the stranger's rudeness, did not flinch under his gaze. Celebrity had done this much for her; it had accustomed her to execrable manners.

"If you do not introduce me to this young lady," the stranger said, "I shall be forced to call you out."

Mogglemere's eyes opened. "Call me out? I haven't insulted you that I recollect, have I? No, now that I think on it, I have said nothing to which you could possibly object. Have I?"

Catherine could not resist a little smile at his lordship's relentless seriousness, and as she smiled, her eyes met the stranger's. He winked at her. "I only used a figure of speech," said the smiling gentleman. "Figures of speech are my métier, you know. Similes, metaphors, all that sort of thing."

Mogglemere frowned, hoping that if he stared the fellow out of countenance, he would go away.

"Introduce me, man," the stranger prompted Mogglemere.

Catherine was pleased then to find herself presented to Lord Byron.

"I have much pleasure in your poetry," she told him as he bowed gracefully over her hand.

"I hope you shall have much more pleasure in the poet," he said.

Appalled at Byron's innuendo, Mogglemere protested. "See here, this is the outside of enough. You have no call to insult the lady."

"Now it is *your* turn to call *me* out," said the poet.

While Mogglemere anxiously pondered a rejoinder, Byron engaged Catherine in conversation and contrived to speak of his travels without making her feel either envious or bored. He was a fine talker and from time to time addressed a question to Lord Mogglemere, which caused the young nobleman to frown and suspect he was being severely quizzed.

Taking pity on Lord Mogglemere, Catherine begged him to procure her a glass of lemonade. At first, he protested, unwilling to leave her in such company, but her pleas and reassurances at last won him over. "I will hurry," he promised, as he went off into the crowd.

"I will apologize in advance for not asking you to dance," said Byron. "You see, I am a cripple. Have been from birth." Here he put out a shapely leg that was hosed in the finest silk and shod in the finest kid. The foot curved inward, as though clubbed. When Catherine looked at his face again, his eyes wore a magnetic expression. She found the gentleman's romantic air enhanced by a hint of tragedy, a suggestion of some heavy grief. Her heart went out to him, and when he winked at her again, she knew he had calculated that it would.

Much as Catherine loved to dance the cotillion, she did not regret her lack of partner. The man who regaled her with tales of his adventures abroad was infinitely more amusing than Lord Mogglemere, and if she could not dance with Sir Rowan, she would prefer to listen to Lord Byron. His poems were fairly equalled by the astonishing power of his eyes, and if she had not already been in love, she might have been in considerable danger.

Byron was too aware of his own charms to permit himself to be overcome by Miss Neville's. He was, however, always on the lookout for a fresh face, and having lived abroad for a time, he had just returned with the intention of pursuing a new flirtation. He had had his fill, for the moment, of European damsels. He was primed for a lady who could understand his sublime words. He knew the world habitually misunderstood the intentions of a brilliant poet, but found that fact highly inconvenient in matters of *amour*. Besides, ladies who communicated by dint of flashing eyes and abandoned sighs had lately begun to weary him. Whereas the month before he had relished the company of women who had the good sense to barter their virtue for trinkets instead of matrimony, he now thought it would be tantalizing to seek the heart of a proper English lady. Catherine Neville, he had decided the moment he set eyes on her, would be the very thing.

When he saw Mogglemere approaching at some distance, Byron quickly promised to call on Miss Neville as soon as he woke up the next day, at six in the evening, most likely. At that time, he vowed, he would bring a poem written in her honour. How he would contrive to write a poem when he meant to sleep away the entire day, he did not explain. Nor did Catherine ask him to, for she thought him wonderfully handsome, breathtakingly brilliant and totally false.

"And now," the poet announced, taking reluctant leave of her, "I shall do you an enormous favour, which will place you forever in my debt."

Here he left her and made his way toward Mogglemere. She watched him cheerfully intercept his lordship, take the glass from his hand and drink the contents. Then, before the young lord could protest that Miss Neville required her lemonade, Byron put his arm through Mogglemere's and, talking to him in the most earnest manner, induced him to walk to one side. There he introduced him to a lady with a musical laugh. Only once did Byron glance at Catherine to see if she observed.

She inclined her head to him, grateful that he had rescued her from the assiduities of Lord Mogglemere, then was immediately recalled to the present by the voice of Sir Rowan. "What the deuce are you doing talking with Byron?" he asked her. "Your reputation will be ruined."

Sweetly, she replied, "You did not ask me to dance. Therefore, I was reduced to scaring up what amusement I could."

"I would have asked you if you had not been rapt in conversation with their lordships."

"Oh, you noticed that, did you? Well, I had had my two dances with Lord Mogglemere, and I could not very well have another. When Lord Byron engaged me in conversation, I could not very well refuse to speak to him. I fear that when it comes to accepting and refusing, a woman has not much choice."

A serious expression crossed his face. "I hope you will accept me when I ask for the honour of having the set after next. And I *do* give you the choice. If you do not wish to accept, I beg you will say so."

"The set after next?"

"I'm afraid I am promised to dance the mazurka with Miss Daphne Perrot. Her mother engineered it. It appears Mr. Omsett was not invited tonight, and I am obliged to stand in for him."

"You need not explain. You are free to do as you like."

"I *was* free to do as I liked. Then I kissed you, and that was the end of that." He strode away upon the announcement of the mazurka, and Catherine was left with the lambent sensation of knowing that he loved her.

She held her arms, as though to contain a sudden electric thrill. She could not continue to stand near the floor. If a gentleman should ask her to dance now, she could not possibly accept. Air was what she required, distance from the crowd, a minute to repeat in her head what Sir Rowan had just said to her.

She found a dark place by a column. Although a crowd of gentlemen stood nearby, the rest of the area was deserted. Leaning against the column, she recreated the sound of Sir Rowan's voice making his stunning declaration. He was not free, he had said. His heart belonged to her. It did not matter who else he danced with. He wanted her. If his words had not made that entirely plain, the warmth in his expression had.

"Calvinia Nutter is her name," said a voice from the crowd of gentlemen.

Hearing her pseudonym mentioned, Catherine looked toward the source, her pleasant thoughts jarred by the sneering tone of the speaker. His voice rang with a familiar irony.

"Read it," the gentlemen cried. "Read it aloud."

"Very well, but you must give me a podium," said the voice. "I cannot be expected to give a reading without a podium."

Suddenly, she saw Lord Byron lifted above the crowd of listeners and carried onto a chair. The gentlemen gathered around to listen. Catherine stepped a little closer, keeping to the dark shadow of the wall so that she might overhear without being seen. She was curious to know what he meant to read and what bearing it could possibly have on Calvinia Nutter.

"From *The Gentleman's Review*," he proclaimed with a flourish of his graceful hand. "And lookee here, it is signed 'A.O.'"

"We all know who that is!" cried a gentleman from the crowd.

"We do indeed," replied Byron. "But he has outdone himself with this item, my friends. Never has our brilliant Mr. A.O. expressed himself with such eloquence, such wit and such taste."

"You mean he praises your verses, most like!" came a taunt from the listeners.

"Be silent, friends, and lend me your fat little ears."

Like the gentleman who stood in rapt anticipation near the poet, Catherine waited. Then she heard as follows:

Of late, the world of letters has been deluged with the sentimental, pious effusions of what have come to be known as "lady poets." Among the newest and most renowned of these exclamatory females is a creature calling herself Calvinia Nutter, and who, if that be her real name, is much to be pitied. However, whether she may also be pardoned for her excess of sensibility and paucity of sense is another matter. She has written a book of sonnets entitled *A Pilgrim's Passion*, though if there be a whit of passion in these lines, I could not detect them. These are crude, rhapsodical verses, such as are too often written in early youth. The poems lack the alchemy needed to transmit emotion that is not only powerful but also genuine. Here we do not have the succinct vigour of poetry but rather mere melodrama and rhetoric. Here, outlandish images substitute for simple, fresh language. In vain does Miss Calvinia Nutter attempt to scale the heights of her art. She cannot surpass the limitations of her sex.

It may be said in Miss Calvinia Nutter's defence that her sonnets jog along rhythmically and her rhymes are genial, if prosaic. But she will have to pattern herself a good deal more after real poets like Byron before she will produce a sure cadence, a precise diction and an objective, broad spirit. I urge her, and her sister "lady poets," to give over the effort. England has need of ladies who attend to their proper affairs and leave the business of writing to those who know something about it. They ought to have no commerce with poetry any more than they should fret their fragile minds with politics, at least not until they can make the music fall eagerly and sweetly from the pen.

CHAPTER SIX

When the hooting and sniggering had died down, Byron was helped from his perch and moved through the crowd. He was surprised to observe Catherine approaching him.

"May I see the review, my lord?" she requested.

He glanced at the paper he held in his hand, then at her face. Seeing her stony look, he complied with her request. So intense was her expression that it roused his curiosity.

It took her some time to read the passage and confirm the reality of such an astonishing attack. Then she looked at Byron and returned the page. "I suppose the gentleman who puts his initials to this review is Mr. Anthony Omsett," she said as calmly as she could.

"I believe it is," Byron answered, searching her face. That she was distressed was evident to him, although a cursory glance at her outward appearance gave the impression that she was as serene as an iceberg. "I did not mean you or any of the ladies to hear this," he said. "You must permit me to apologize for any expressions that may have offended you and your sex." Although she avoided meeting his eyes, he could tell that hers were full.

Quietly, Catherine said, "You did not write this viciousness, my lord. Therefore, there is no need for you to apologize."

Despite her words, he might have attempted further apologies had she not turned and moved toward a nearby arch. He seized her hand, attempting to stop her. "Wait," he urged her. "You must tell me what has overset you."

Too numb to reply, Catherine glanced emptily at the hand he held. Something about the glacial tranquillity of her aspect impelled him to drop the hand. Slowly she disappeared through the arch, and all the poet could do was stare after her. Suddenly, he was taken by the shoulders and spun around.

"What the deuce have you been saying to Miss Neville?" Sir Rowan demanded.

Byron lifted his hands in protest. "I have said nothing to her, I take my oath."

"I saw what happened. You tried to take her hand and she was forced to rebuff you."

"You are mistaken, Heath. That is not what happened. I am not sure myself what happened."

Sir Rowan did not stay to hear Lord Byron attempt to explain his exchange with Miss Neville. He strode through the arch, determined to find her.

The arch led to a landing from which a staircase curled in two directions. He took the steps that led upward and soon found himself on the balcony. He scoured it, searching the faces of the young ladies, startling them by staring into their eyes, then looking thoroughly dissatisfied at what he beheld. Near the corner where the two balconies met, he found a door, and seeing it slightly ajar, he opened it and went inside. There he found a lady of his acquaintance kissing a gentleman who was not her husband. "Damn!" Sir Rowan muttered, causing the lady to spring from her lover's lap and cry out in terror.

"Carry on," the baronet said impatiently and bowed swiftly out of the room.

Taking the stairs once again, he briskly descended to the gallery which led to the principal entrance. Not far from four liveried footmen standing at attention by the door sat Catherine, dwarfed by an enormous, ancient chair of wood and black leather. Her white-knuckled hands gripped the arms of the chair; her eyes were fixed on a point in space. The sight of her caused him to stop.

It was clear to him that something or someone had sent the colour flying from her cheeks. Not for a minute did he believe Byron's protestations of innocence, and he would so inform the fellow when he got his hands on him. Lord Byron was a brute. He was no sooner finished seducing one female than he looked to ruin another. But if he had any idea of harming Miss Neville, Sir Rowan would be delighted to teach him to think otherwise.

CATHERINE WAS TOO ABSORBED in thought to see Sir Rowan. It struck her that Mr. Omsett's review was so out of proportion in its contempt as to be remarkable. Such venom could not be inspired by her poems, however lame they might be. Such venom could spring only from one of two sources: the man was either too callous to regard the cruelty of his words, or else he had been perfectly aware of his cruelty and had persevered anyway. She had heard of such gentlemen, but until now, she had never believed in their existence.

She looked up to see Sir Rowan approaching, as though in answer to her desperate wish. For a moment she could not believe he was real. A well of gratitude flushed over her when she read the concern on his face.

"May I get you a glass of wine, send for your servant perhaps?" he enquired.

His speaking indicated that he was indeed real. "Would you kindly see me to Curzon Street?" she asked. "I do not wish to trouble Lady Perrot."

He instructed one of the servants to fetch his carriage and the other to inform her ladyship that as Miss Neville had been taken ill, he had escorted her to Perrot House. In the space of a few minutes, they were ensconced in Sir Rowan's carriage, coursing through the dark streets, bouncing at every pothole and rocking with the swaying motion.

"Look here, Catherine," said the baronet when he had had as much silence as he could withstand. "Whatever Byron said, I urge you to pay it no heed. He makes a point of offending ladies whenever he can. He considers it part and parcel of his charm. Oblige me, if you would, and do not give him the satisfaction of seeing you offended."

She looked up at him, then closed her eyes. Seeing her shiver, he felt an impulse to hold her. All at once, she threw herself on his chest, so that her hair brushed his cheek and he could breathe her fragrance. "What is it?" he murmured, folding his arms around her. "What has made you so unhappy?"

"I am not unhappy," she whispered into his lapel. "I am furious."

He could not resist a smile. "Oh, is that all."

Lifting her head, she told him with glistening eyes, "I shall make him sorry for this. You will see."

"Simple country girls do not go about wreaking revenge. It is decidedly outré this season." He allowed his fingers to smooth a wisp of blond curl from her cheek.

"If I were Miss Perrot, I might remind you of the saying that revenge is sweet." She did not move away, lest he take his arm from her shoulder.

"And if I were Lord Mogglemere, I should be solicitous of your muse and warn you that talk of anything so disagreeable as revenge might incite her to pack her trunks and go off in a snit."

"What shall I talk of, then?"

He took her hand and brought it to his lips. "Don't talk at all," he suggested, then pressed her to him and kissed her. She could not tell whether it was the noise of the carriage wheels or the whirring of her brain that sang to her, but she felt herself suddenly light and musical. The weight that had oppressed her now lifted. Her hands moved from his lapel to his face, so that she might touch him with as much urgency as his mouth sought her neck. She felt herself emit a cry of joy that was swallowed up in the London traffic noise and answered by aching whispers in her ear.

Too soon they reached Curzon Street, where they were forced to delay their descent from the carriage in order to rearrange their persons and collect their emotions. Finally Sir Rowan stepped out, then handed Catherine out, resisting an urge to kiss her on the street in full view of footmen, coachman and tiger. There was no opportunity to linger at the door, for it was immediately opened by the butler, who stood at attention, waiting for the lady to enter.

"You did not dance with me this evening," Sir Rowan reminded her. "I mean to collect what is owed to me tonight."

"I hope you do not mean to dance with me in Curzon Street. Weeks would be shocked, wouldn't you, Weeks?" she asked the butler.

"As you wish, madam," he replied coolly.

"Weeks," said the baronet. "You may go and tell Miss Neville's maid that she has come back."

"Miss Neville's maid is in readiness for her mistress, I assure you, sir."

"In that case, Weeks, you may go and ask my coachman to walk the horses until I am ready to be driven home."

The butler, glancing through the open door into the street, observed, "Your coachman is already walking the horses, sir."

Narrowing his eyes, the baronet said, "Weeks, you may go to the devil, at least until I have taken proper leave of Miss Neville."

"Ah, you wish to be rid of me, sir." Here the butler nodded and vanished into an anteroom. Sir Rowan took one look at the coachman, footmen, and tiger who grinned at him from the street and threw the door shut. With privacy thus assured, he was able to draw Catherine to him and caress her with his lips. "I shall not insist that you dance with me here and now if you will agree to favour another request of mine."

She smiled up at him archly, "My dear sir, I do not know whether I can relinquish that dance. I looked forward to it nearly as much as I looked forward to your lecture on the swans, and I have been disappointed in both."

He held her away and regarded her. "Joke if you will, but I am perfectly serious. I want to marry you."

She felt her eyes fill and could not imagine why she should be on the point of tears when she had never felt so happy in her life.

"I know you love me. Say you will have me."

"You are awfully sure of yourself, Sir Rowan. How do you know I love you?"

"Because you were jealous of my attentions to Miss Perrot, for which I thank you with all my heart."

She blushed. "How could you know I was jealous? I hardly knew it myself."

"Catherine, marry me. If you say you will be my wife, you will never want for swan lectures or dances."

"But we have not even known one another a month."

"Time enough to learn that I love you."

This declaration stopped her for a moment, and she could not help smiling at him and sighing. Much as she cherished his love, however, she could not forbear saying, "I'm afraid this offer is prompted by your much-lamented carelessness, rather than reason. Surely we ought to better our acquaintance before plunging into matrimony."

"Marry me and then we shall have every opportunity of bettering our acquaintance."

Laughing, she said, "I am no match for your sophistry. I have done what I may to be rational in this matter and it has done no good. Therefore, I have no other course but to agree to marry you." Shyly, she touched his cheek and brushed his lips with her own.

Their farewell at last inspired the baronet to vow they should be married at once, by special licence. During this scene, the butler peeked his nose out several times, and finding that the young miss was still absorbed in goodbyes, he was compelled to cool his heels for a while longer. At last, the baronet was induced by his lady love to take his leave, Miss Neville retired above stairs with many a sigh, and the butler was permitted to resume his post before the family returned.

CATHERINE HAPPENED TO GLANCE in the glass as the maid undressed her and noticed that her face wore a decidedly daft expression. She laughed out loud at the sight, enjoying it, revelling in it, and sighing again and again. The maid, who had seen many a young lady comport herself in such a manner after a ball, shook her head cynically. Only one thing followed such raptures, in her experience—a broken heart. Consequently, she proceeded to warn Catherine in the most dire accents to be on her guard. But Catherine heard nary a word, for her imagination had transported her once again to the baronet's carriage, where she was again jounced and kissed and jostled and held.

Turning down the sheets, the maid installed her lady in the bed, took up the candle and tiptoed out, mourning in advance for the suffering in store for poor Miss Neville. Miss Neville, meanwhile, cared not a farthing for any suffering, but hugged herself deliciously and reconciled herself to getting not a wink the entire night.

So many ideas filled her head that she did not know which she ought to think of first. She must write to her sister Anne with the news of her engagement. She must acquire wedding clothes. She must learn who Sir Rowan's family were and which of them she would be expected to meet straightaway. She must grow used to being a ladyship, and she must enquire of Anne how a married woman was expected to behave on her honeymoon.

No unpleasant thought obtruded on these musings until it occurred to her that Miss Perrot would be made dreadfully unhappy by the announcement of Sir Rowan's engagement to herself. Catherine spent considerable time regretting that her happiness would cause grief to another, and she devoutly hoped that the young woman would waste no time in scaring up an elegant extract with which to console herself.

From this melancholy idea, her mind jumped to one a good deal more distressing: namely, Mr. Anthony Omsett's review of *A Pilgrim's Passion*. She had never deceived herself that her sonnets rivalled the poetry of Byron; nor had she ever nurtured the foolish hope that everyone who read her poems would find them to their liking. But she had thought that Mr. Omsett was fair-minded and moderate. In the time she had conversed with him at Lady Perrot's party, she found him intelligent, respectful and not at all given to vitriolic opinions. During the entire outing in St. James's Park, he had shown himself the gentlest and mildest of men. How could such a man pen such a review? How could he smile at her and exchange polite nothings with her, knowing what he had written about her and her book? How could he use her poor poems as a pretext for attacking the understanding, skill and dignity of the entire female sex?

Catherine punched her pillows several times before sitting up in her bed and making a decision. The very next day, she would pay a visit to the chambers of *The Gentleman's Review*. She would put to Mr. Anthony Omsett the very same questions that troubled her, and she would see whether he had anything, anything at all, to say in his own defence.

AFTER LEAVING CATHERINE, Sir Rowan tapped on the roof of the carriage with his horse-head walking stick. The coachman drew up and was instructed not to drive to the baronet's house in Berkeley Square, but rather to the lodgings of Lord Byron. Shortly thereafter, he was deposited at a fine, modern building in Belgravia. There the baronet climbed the stairs and knocked. Byron's man opened the door and informed Sir Rowan that his lordship had not yet returned.

"I shall wait," said the baronet, brushing past the man and letting himself into the luxurious sitting room. He looked round at the assortment of exotic paintings, statues and hangings strewn about the walls, tables and floor, and did what he could to make himself comfortable on a sofa masquerading as a cloud of cushions. The man brought Sir Rowan a bottle and a glass, set them near him on a table, and went to bed.

It was noon before Byron made his appearance. Noisily, he entered his lodgings in the company of three young women to whom he was teaching an Italian song. When he saw Sir Rowan, he stopped, swayed a little drunkenly, and invited the baronet to partake of the young ladies with him. "I am not selfish," he assured Sir Rowan, falling onto the sofa beside him and resting his head on his shoulder. "Of all things, I most abhor selfishness. You shall have the little one, the one with the mole. I shall have the other two. I have no difficulty making do with two. Good God, *do* and *two*—what an execrable rhyme!"

Sir Rowan took the poet by the hair and removed his head from his shoulder. He then fixed the young women with a firm eye, which caused them to cease laughing and to shift about uncomfortably. "You will excuse his lordship a moment," said the baronet, and eyed them as they took themselves off to another room, with which they were evidently familiar.

Turning to his companion again, he found Lord Byron fast asleep. He permitted himself the pleasure of waking the poet with several smart smacks to the cheek.

"I must rest," Byron murmured, his head lolling back and forth.

"Not until you tell me what took place between you and Miss Neville."

Sloppily, Byron grinned. "Ah, Miss Neville. A delectable morsel that. What is she to you?"

"I mean to marry her."

This astonishing revelation succeeded in opening Byron's eyes. "Marry? You? Never! You are too fond of making political enemies to have time for the fair sex. And what female in possession of her faculties would have you?"

"Miss Neville has said she will have me, which is one reason I am here. You are not to trouble her further with your attentions. Is that understood?"

Byron summoned his dignity and rose, catching himself before sinking onto the sofa again. "I never 'trouble' anyone with my attentions. My attentions are always welcome, I assure you. In the case of Miss Neville, I might have favoured her with a mild flirtation, but she fell into an unaccountable dejection and went away before I could work my charms."

"You tried to seduce her, and in disgust, she was forced to leave the ball."

"I never did anything of the kind," Byron shouted, then put a hand to his head. "I must remember not to shout," he whispered. "It is the devil of a head I am wearing tonight—I mean today."

Sir Rowan stood up. "I see I won't get anything from you this day. I shall come back when you are coherent."

"Wait," Byron said. "You have wronged me, Heath, and you cannot leave until you apologize. I do not mind being vilified for seductions I have committed, but I will not be blamed for those I have not yet accomplished."

"You are drunk. I'll return another time."

Byron seized Sir Rowan by the lapel and said, "No, no. I am innocent here, and you shall know it. What happened was this: I was reading aloud from a review I happened to notice in Lord Tristram's private sitting room. You will not ask me what I was doing in his private sitting room, if you please, for I was accompanied by a lady whose reputation will be sullied beyond repair if I mention her name. Besides, I do not recall her name. In any case, the lady was in a pet and would not speak to me, so there was nothing for it but to read until she changed her mind. I was struck by a piece in the thing, a delightfully poisonous piece it was, and so I tore the page out and took it with me when I returned to the ballroom. Soon afterward, the opportunity presented itself for me to read it aloud to a select group of gentlemen. I did not wish the ladies to hear it, for the author made sundry observations that must tweak the pride of any female above the age of four. But despite my precautions, I fear Miss Neville overheard me, because she asked to see the review afterward and appeared much shaken by it."

"You are speaking gibberish. What review? Show it to me."

"Good heavens, do you think I carry such a thing on my person?"

When Sir Rowan gave a look of disgust and moved to leave, Byron seized his coat again and said, "Wait, perhaps I do carry it on my person. One is not always aware of what one carries on one's person." He thereupon searched his pockets and, along with a lady's comb, a lock of hair and a stocking, brought out a crumpled bit of paper that proved to be the review of *A Pilgrim's Passion*. "Aha!" he cried triumphantly. "We are in luck."

Sir Rowan unfolded the paper, and as he read the review he had written for Tony Omsett, his lips thinned into a grim line.

"An unfortunate piece," Byron lamented. "The very last thing one ought to call the lady poets is 'lady poets.' They hate it above everything."

"This is unconscionable," said the baronet hoarsely.

"I would not go so far as to say that," protested Byron. "It is an amusing piece, stylistically superior to what one generally reads in such reviews. Most of all, it has feeling. That is what I like about it—there is a fund of passion behind it. One would not think old Tony Omsett capable of such depth of passion. He is well enough, of course, but he is a bland sort of fellow, not much in the passion line, I have always thought. I myself have more than a little experience in that regard, and I fancy myself able to recognize a brother when I see one. I never suspected old Tony of being of the fraternity."

Here the young ladies poked their heads out the door and in singsong voices complained of his lordship's neglect.

"You may arrange a tableau while you are waiting," he called to them. "I wish to see Aphrodite, Athena and Atalanta netting a purse." When they closed the door again, he whispered to Sir Rowan, "Now that ought to keep them occupied for a bit."

The baronet had paid little attention to anything Byron had said since he had read the review. His thoughts were preoccupied with the perversity of events, with the throttling he would give Tony Omsett, and with the unforgivable wound he had carelessly inflicted on the woman he wished to marry. With an effort, he contained his anger. He crumpled the paper into a ball and placed it in Byron's palm.

"I see that you do not like the review, Heath. You look as pale as Miss Neville did."

"I beg your pardon, Byron. I accused you unjustly."

"No matter. It is a novelty to be accused unjustly of seducing a young lady. But what is there in this piece that seems to cause such universal distress? Do you disagree with the reviewer's opinion? Have you actually read the volume of which he writes? Do you have a copy I might borrow?"

Sir Rowan inclined his head in a short bow. "I will leave you now. Forgive me for taking up so much of your time at such an hour."

Before he could make his exit, Byron cried out, "I know what it is! I smoke it!"

The baronet turned, dreading what he might hear.

Byron approached, grinning wickedly and shaking a finger at him. "You know this Miss Calvinia Nutter, do you not? You know who she is, and so, I'll warrant, does Miss Neville."

"Good morning to you, Byron," said the baronet, walking from the room. To his irritation, Byron followed.

"Your Miss Nutter will be grievously pained by this review, will she not? Even I, thick-skinned as I am, have felt the sting of the critic's barb. I daresay the lady will never speak to Tony Omsett again as long as she lives."

Sir Rowan set his jaw. Declining to answer, he showed himself out the door, headed down the stairs, and stepped into his carriage.

Meanwhile, Byron thought it odd that a review of a new book of poems should excite so much interest, especially as they were not *his* poems. He therefore unfolded the ball of paper he held and settled into his cloud of cushions to have another look.

CHAPTER SEVEN

WHILE THE OTHER LADIES of the household slept the morning away, Catherine sat alone in the breakfast parlour, enjoying a second helping of sausage and toast. She had awakened with a vigorous appetite, which she meant to appease fully before setting forth to see Mr. Omsett. She could not be wholly out of charity with the young man. After all, he obviously suffered from an excess of spleen, owing no doubt to the fact that he was not wildly and deliciously in love—as he ought to be, as everyone ought to be. Once Miss Daphne Perrot or some other fair damsel captured what little heart he could claim to possess, he would be forced to reform his unfeeling ways. He would then have the wherewithal to review a book like a sensible man.

These musings were interrupted by the appearance of Miss Philippa Perrot who, though looking groggy from the previous night's exertions, entered with an air of purpose. Helping herself to a morsel from the sideboard, Miss Perrot sat next to Catherine and said, "I am so glad to have found you alone. I have something particular to say to you and guessed that you would be the only one breakfasting. A country upbringing appears to imbue one with appetite in the morning."

Her curiosity roused, Catherine watched expectantly as the young woman's coffee was served out by the footman. After sipping, Philippa said, "I wish to ask your advice, Miss Neville."

As her opinion had not often been sought, much less her advice, Catherine felt more curious than ever.

"I have heard what my mother and my sister have to say on the thorny subject I bring before you," Miss Perrot continued, "but they are prejudiced, you see. I must have the advice of a more objective observer, and you, Miss Neville, are not only objective, being an outsider, but you are also a keen observer. Nay, you could not write so poetically if you were not."

"I shall do my best to advise you, but then, I'm afraid, I must leave you. I have an important errand in Fleet Street."

"In that case, I shall make haste. My situation, briefly, is this—I am advised on all sides not to speak when in the company of Sir Rowan Heath. It has been brought home to me that he will dislike it if he hears me converse; whereas, if I am silent, he will like it so very much that he will make me an offer of marriage."

Catherine flushed.

"Ah, I see by the colour in your cheeks that you find the idea of deception as distasteful as I do. Indeed, should I continue to be silent in his presence, I fear I shall be forced to declare with Thomas Otway: 'Destructive, damnable, deceitful woman!' You will, I know, excuse my saying 'damnable,' as it is part of the quotation."

"I do not know what to tell you," Catherine replied. She was reluctant to pain the young woman by blurting out the truth.

"It was not many weeks ago that Sir Rowan sat with me in this very house and we discussed a great many subjects. As I recall, I alluded to Shakespeare. He did not appear in the least disgusted, nor did he flee my company afterward.''

"He does not strike me as a man likely to be driven off by a little Shakespeare,'' Catherine stated.

"Precisely. Furthermore, I do not see why I should pretend to be other than what I am.''

"I am sure Sir Rowan would not wish you to put yourself to so much trouble for his sake.''

"That is what I think. He is truly manly in that regard.''

Catherine nodded her agreement.

"Good. Then it is your opinion that if I do not conceal my facility for extraction and that if I do make use of a quotation now and again, the gentleman will still offer for me.''

"Oh, dear,'' Catherine said. "I cannot say in truth that I believe he will offer for you. You see, the gentleman has already offered for someone else.''

Philippa raised her brows. "Impossible, Miss Neville. Sir Rowan and I were on the best of terms last night. I do believe he means to propose very soon, if not today.''

Inhaling, Catherine answered, "I am very sorry to have to distress you, Miss Perrot, but Sir Rowan and I are engaged.''

"Sir Rowan and you?'' Philippa stood up, knocking over her coffee cup.

"I'm afraid so.''

"But you are to have Lord Mogglemere!''

"I beg your pardon, but it was *you* who was to have Lord Mogglemere.''

Philippa pouted. "But I don't like Lord Mogglemere.''

"I am very sorry you are disappointed,'' Catherine said.

Miss Perrot's voice rose. "I felt certain Sir Rowan meant to propose to me. Mama said he would, and even Daphne thought he was most attentive. Oh, heavens, I ought to have known he was only being polite, that I read more into his attentions than was meant. It is not his fault if he is the gentlest, kindest, most gallant gentleman on the face of this earth."

Catherine rose. Moved by the young woman's heart-felt admiration for Sir Rowan, she took her hand. "You will find a husband some day who loves you exactly as you are. You will not need to keep silent or refrain from quoting to be noticed."

Biting her lip, Philippa withdrew her hand swiftly from Catherine's. "You will excuse me, I hope," she said in a tone of barely suppressed resentment. Turning, she walked to the door.

"Miss Perrot. Philippa," Catherine cried. "I hope you will wish me happy."

The young lady stopped to declare, "As Lady Heath, you are sure to be happy. You do not need my blessing."

"But I should like to continue to have your friendship."

Philippa eyed her coldly. "You have engaged yourself to the man I ought to have married, the only one I could love and live happily with. That knowledge will have to satisfy you. You cannot demand my friendship as well. Now I must excuse myself. I find I am not very hungry and do not want breakfast."

When she had tottered from the room, Catherine found that her appetite was gone as well.

AT THE CHAMBERS of *The Gentleman's Review*, Mr. Omsett was in excellent spirits. The recent edition had been brought out on time. Furthermore, Mr. Wolley, the publisher, had remarked that the coffee-house talk was full of its brilliance, and he had congratulated him upon it. Tony was on the point of settling down at his desk to compose an essay for the new issue, when Miss Neville was announced.

"Desire her to come in," he told the clerk.

Catherine entered, glanced about at the cluttered room, and took the chair that was offered her. She wore a green silk bonnet which bobbed its plume as she leaned forward and prepared to speak. "I'm afraid I do not come on a pleasant errand."

Tony regarded her with alarm. "Good God," he cried, "it is Miss Daphne Perrot. She is ill. You have come to summon me to her side. I shall come at once."

Catherine shook her head. "Miss Daphne Perrot enjoys the very best of health."

He leaned back in his chair, sighing in relief. "Have you brought me an invitation, then? If so, I must thank you for delivering it in person. I am honoured to be visited by a lady of such beauty as well as poetical gifts."

"You need not pretend with me, sir. I know you are not an admirer of my poetical gifts, or those of my sister poets."

He sat up in his chair and stared at her. "I cannot imagine what leads you to such a conclusion. If my manners have been at fault, I beg leave to apologize."

Catherine rolled her eyes. "This is foolishness, sir. I know you are the one who wrote the review of *A Pilgrim's Passion*."

Tony regarded her with genuine bafflement. Her bouncing hat feather waved at him like a pointing finger.

Firmly, Catherine went on, "I am obliged to remind you that I am Calvinia Nutter. I am stunned at what you have written and the viciousness with which you have written it. I demand an explanation."

"An explanation?" he rasped.

"You are Mr. A.O., are you not?"

"I suppose I am."

"And you are the author of this, are you not?" Here she seized the copy of *The Gentleman's Review* which lay before him. Turning to the page she sought, she threw it on his desk so that he might read it.

He looked down uncomprehendingly. After a time, the words and sentences began to come into focus. As he read, his jaw fell open and his complexion grew white. Looking up in a fright, he said to Catherine, "He will murder me!"

At the sight of such terror, Catherine could not help but sympathize. "I am sure your publisher will not murder you," she said with more gentleness than she intended, "although, I confess, I had every intention of doing so myself."

"Please do not be angry with me."

"I am very angry, but I am determined to hear you out. I should have understood if you wrote that you did not like my poems and did so honestly, with a due reverence for the art of poetry. But I cannot understand why you excoriated my work so cruelly—and the work of every female poet, both living and dead."

"Heaven help me, did I do that?"

"Mr. Omsett, you know you did."

"Oh, this is dreadful, dreadful."

"I don't suppose that very many authors have charged into your chambers in order to give you a scold. But if you do not mend your ways, sir, you will have to get used to it."

"It will not matter. He will kill me before I have the chance to get used to it."

"I am certain you overstate the case. I do not know Mr. Wolley except by reputation, but I am certain he will take your youth into account. In any case, you have not answered my question; nor have you given me any hint as to how a gentleman who appears as mild and refined as you do can write such savagery."

"I only wrote what I wrote, Miss Neville, because . . . it seemed to be the thing to do at the time."

"That explanation will not do, sir."

"It is rather lame, isn't it?"

"How can you behave so charmingly to me and then write such things? How is it possible that a man can be so two-faced?"

Tony looked desperately about the room, as though the answer might be found tacked to the wall or hanging from the ceiling. "Well, one cannot go about in drawing rooms and ballrooms speaking savagery, as you put it. One would be cut everywhere and have no friends left. A review, on the other hand, is useless if it is merely charming. If one is honest, showing all due reverence for the art of poetry, one's readers will be bored beyond bearing and refuse to read it."

"Do you mean to say that you wrote this merely to appease what you imagine to be your readers' taste?"

Wretchedly, the young man replied, "That appears to be what I mean."

Catherine stood and moved to the door. "I am disappointed, Mr. Omsett. I had thought better of you." She placed her hand on the doorknob, preparing to leave.

Mortified, Tony replied, "Please do not hate me altogether, I beg you. If I had read your poems, I am certain I would have written far differently."

Whipping around she cried, "You mean you wrote that poison without reading the book?"

"Yes. I assure you, when I did read it, I found the poems quite tolerable. You will be gratified to know that not a particle of the opinions expressed in this review emanate from any actual reading of your work."

Too appalled to speak, Catherine inhaled and opened the door. With her back still to him, she said, "You will oblige me, sir, by not speaking to me or appearing to know me whenever we are so unlucky as to be in company together. I do not wish to be acquainted with a gentleman who writes such attacks without even reading the work he is attacking; nor can I consider such a mean-spirited, dishonest writer a gentleman. Good day to you." On this, she marched from the chamber.

Tony then put his head in his hands, moaned piteously once or twice, called on heaven to take him before Sir Rowan sent him there and then reread the piece to assure himself that the wrong review had indeed been printed. Half an hour later, when Sir Rowan Heath was announced, the young man still sat with his head in his hands.

Warily, Tony observed the baronet's entrance. Sir Rowan tapped his horse-head walking stick against his gloved hand, glancing only once at his friend. Having nothing to say for himself, Tony slunk down in his chair, an admission of guilt that the baronet answered by pointing the ivory horse head at the review open on the desk and banging it down thunderously, so that Tony was forced to clap his hands to his ears.

"Go ahead, beat me," he implored Sir Rowan. "I deserve it."

Sir Rowan could not beat a man who displayed such remorse. He therefore sat in the chair lately vacated by

Catherine, and asked simply, "What the devil happened?"

"I printed the wrong review."

Sir Rowan nodded his head. "So I see. What I don't see is how you came to do such a thing."

Nearly at the point of tears, Tony cried, "I don't know."

"You recall that when I placed the second review in your hand, I instructed you to take it directly to the printer."

"Yes, of course, I remember. It was the day after we were at Perrot House. You said you did not wish me to print the review you had written the night before. Then you handed me another review to replace it. I recall, I put the review in the pocket of my coat, so that I would remember to deliver it to the printer. I take my oath, Heath, I recollect the incident as though it happened yesterday. I then put the paper you gave me right here, under my paper knife, so that I would not forget it." Here he threw aside the paper knife, which sat on a stack of papers, and saw something that caused him to swallow. His face contorted into an expression of horror as he reached for it. There in his hand lay the second review Sir Rowan had penned.

"Thank you, Tony. Now I know what the devil happened."

Limply, Mr. Omsett asked, "What is to be done?"

"I don't know. Miss Neville has read it. I'm afraid she was a good deal distressed by it last night."

"She was a good deal distressed today as well."

Sir Rowan sat up. "She was here?"

"Indeed she was, and demanding explanations."

"What did you tell her?"

"I hardly know. I was so stunned by what I had done that I could not adjust my thoughts. I doubt I made any sense at all."

"Did you tell her that I wrote the review?"

"I don't think so."

"Tony, I don't wish you to lie for me."

"I didn't lie. I simply didn't tell the truth."

"I will not have you taking the blame for this review. It was my carelessness which caused the trouble to begin with, and so I will tell her."

"I don't advise you to tell her, Heath. She was fierce enough with me. She will not be any gentler with you."

"I think she will be. You see, she has agreed to marry me."

Tony gasped. "You? Married? Impossible. Next you will be telling me that Byron has been named Archbishop of Canterbury."

"I asked her to marry me last night, and she accepted."

"Then you must under no circumstances tell her the truth. It is imperative that you let me shoulder the blame."

"No."

"If you are revolted at the idea, I shall allow you to pay me a little something for my trouble."

Sir Rowan stood up. "I have no doubt you would allow me to pay you, old fellow, but I prefer not to embark on the sea of matrimony in a vessel constructed of lies."

"Your metaphor is very pretty, Heath, but, if I may be permitted to expand upon it, it does not hold water. Miss Neville will break your engagement the instant she hears the truth. Oh, I know, you think she loves you too much to be so angry as to jilt you. She does not appear to you to be unforgiving. Nor do you believe that she is so unreasonably sensitive with respect to her poems that she would not see the justification, the absurdity, even the humour in what we did that fateful evening. But I promise you, she will hate you for it. If you had seen the fire in her eyes when she was here, you would know it as well as I do. Be warned, my friend. Do not make the situation worse by confessing. In this case, as in all cases, it is best to abide by the principle of never confessing anything to a female. If you disregard this excellent wisdom, you had best be prepared to regret it the rest of your life.''

WHEN CATHERINE RETURNED to Curzon Street, she found the ladies of the house awaiting her in the sitting room. Philippa sat in a straight-backed chair, her mother stood behind the chair with her hands protectively on her daughter's shoulders and Daphne lounged on a sofa, yawning.

"Is this true what my daughter tells me, Miss Neville?" asked her ladyship in ominous tones. "You are engaged to Sir Rowan?"

Catherine saw the dark looks on the faces of the mother and daughter and hesitated before answering that yes, it was true.

Daphne fidgeted with her curls. "I told you it must be true, Mama. You expected Sir Rowan to offer for Philippa simply because she fainted in his arms and he caught her, but any gentleman worth a groat would have done the same thing, except Lord Mogglemere, of course. He would not have the wit."

"It is not merely because I fainted in his arms!" Philippa cried. "He danced the first two dances with me last night. What have you to say to that, I should like to know?"

"What I have to say is this," her sister retorted, "that I danced the first two with the brigadier, who has a goiter and a toothless smile. You do not see me pining after marrying him, do you? Nor do you see him proposing to me. You thought Sir Rowan would propose because you wished to, and now you have got exactly what you deserve."

"Lord, save me from sisterly consolation," Philippa moaned.

"Is that one of your nasty quotations?" Daphne sniffed. "It is no wonder Sir Rowan preferred Miss Neville. At least she does not prose at him."

"I did not prose at Sir Rowan. You told me I must keep quiet, and keep quiet I did, for all the good it accomplished."

Here Lady Perrot interceded, quieted her daughters and addressed Catherine, who had waited in dread for the sisters to cease arguing with each other and direct their wrath at her.

"Is this how you repay my hospitality, Miss Neville?" her ladyship asked in a low voice. "If my health permitted, I should spend the next hours explaining to you your obligations to a family who have taken you in and franked your expenses out of the purest and most disinterested friendship."

"Uncle Binky franks her expenses, Mama," Daphne pointed out.

"Have we done something to provoke your resentment?" enquired her ladyship in a tone of profound hurt. "Did you set out to rob Philippa of her prospects because of some vendetta you have conceived against us— for what reason I cannot imagine?"

Catherine would have reminded Lady Perrot of her usefulness to the family in the past, of her promise to stay on until Miss Perrot had won Lord Mogglemere's heart and hand, of the sacrifice she had made of her own wishes in order to gratify her ladyship's request that she stay in London, but Weeks appeared then to announce that Miss Neville had a visitor. Grateful for the excuse to escape, Catherine followed the butler from the sitting room to the day parlour.

The visitor proved to be Lord Byron, who, the instant Catherine entered, assumed a look of ardent sympathy. "I had to come see how you do today. I'm afraid you were not well when you left Tristram House last night." He seemed unaware that he had taken possession of her hand and held it to his breast.

Catherine, who was very much aware of what had become of her hand, endeavoured to pull it away, but it would not come. "I am well enough, my lord. I should do a great deal better if you gave me back my hand."

"I cannot do that." He appeared too troubled to meet her eyes with his smouldering brown ones. Therefore, he turned his magnificent profile to her and stared broodingly at a painted plate on the mantel.

"I should like to know why you cannot give me my hand."

"Because I have been thinking about you every minute since you left me. I have not slept a wink this night, thinking about you and what sent you flying from me nearly in tears. And I have reached certain conclusions."

"I do not see what all this has to do with my hand."

"I conclude that the review I read to my companions distressed you because you were nearly concerned in its subject. In short, you are Miss Calvinia Nutter. Am I right?"

Catherine swallowed hard. "I have never tried to conceal my identity."

"I knew you could not feel the many slights contained in that piece so profoundly if you had not been the author referred to. Believe me, I do not regard it lightly when I am reviewed unfairly by a clot who would not recognize poetry if he stubbed his toe on it. I know precisely how you feel." He pressed her hand more urgently to his bosom, but she did not notice, so fascinated was she by the man's accuracy of conjecture.

"I thank you for your understanding, my lord. I had not expected it."

"Do you think me an insensible clot, too?"

"No, you are only a flirt."

This disconcerted the gentleman considerably. "A flirt? You thought I was only flirting with you last night?"

She smiled. "Yes."

He could not help admiring her more than ever. His suspicion that a proper English miss would be a good deal more amusing than any of the demi-reps and dancers he had frequented of late had been pure inspiration. This Miss Neville—Miss Calvinia Nutter—would be the sweetest dish he had tasted in many a month. He would have to have a look at her poetry soon so that he might flatter her knowledgeably. In the past, he had used his own poetry to seduce young women. Now he relished the novelty of using the young woman's own poetry for the same purpose.

In addition to reading her sonnets, he would have to teach himself to be patient. This young woman was no fool; she would not be easily bamboozled. She would not be rushed. He must bide his time. But before he did any of these deeds, he must set the stage, which he proceeded to do by saying, "I have come to another conclusion, my dear lady." This time he looked straight into her eyes, with an expression so liquid and so heated that she was riveted.

A little breathlessly, she said, "What is it?"

"It is this—the author of the review cannot be Mr. Omsett. It can be none other than Sir Rowan Heath."

CHAPTER EIGHT

SIR ROWAN REPAIRED to Child's in St. Paul's Churchyard. The coffeehouse smelled pungently of pipe tobacco and brandy. Sir Rowan took a large, comfortable chair near the fire, where a number of gentlemen read newspapers and smoked, and endeavoured to compose a confession.

Ordinarily the baronet would have sat at one of the small tables, talking to men of his acquaintance about political matters of the day. The heat of argument combined with the hum of conviviality always animated him. Invariably he would be inspired to call for pen and paper so that he might jot down the satiric jibes that came into his head. Today, in contrast, he was not inspired to call for pen and paper.

At first, he had thought it might be best to write the confession and send it to Catherine in the form of a letter. Then he recollected that his writing was what had pained her to begin with, and so he reconciled himself to telling her the truth to her lovely face. "My dear Catherine," he began in his thoughts over and over again. "My dearest Catherine. My beloved Catherine." He could not get beyond the salutation. What more could he say that did not damn him as a careless fellow?

"Sir Rowan," said Lord Mogglemere. "Now this is amazingly convenient, is it not?"

The baronet did not see that it was in the least convenient to be interrupted in his thoughts by such a one as Lord Mogglemere. Thus, he eyed the gentleman coolly. This reception was invitation enough for his lordship, who sat down in a vacant chair close by.

"I have been thinking all morning how to phrase something I've had knocking about in my brain," Mogglemere confided, "and I vow you are the very man to help me."

Seeing that his lordship's case bore a similarity to his own, Sir Rowan grew curious. "What is it you are trying to phrase?" he asked. "Can it be that you have resolved to write a letter to the *Times*?"

His lordship laughed. "I? Write a letter to the *Times*? Why, I can barely string six words together. No, I leave the scribbling to such as you and Miss Neville. What I have in mind is another sort of matter." Here he raised and lowered his red eyebrows significantly.

Sir Rowan smiled at the travelling brows. Perhaps Mogglemere would be of service in amusing him, thus clearing his mind for the ordeal ahead.

"You know how to turn a phrase neatly," his lordship said, "and so I thought I might ask your advice."

The reference to "turning a phrase neatly" caused the baronet some uneasiness. It had recently come home to him most painfully that too much cleverness of expression could undo a fellow. He paused before saying, "I shall endeavour to advise you as best I can, as long as you do not ask me to write a review."

"Heavens, no. What I have in mind is not intended to be written. It is to be spoken. By me." He cleared his throat.

"All the better. I have a little speech of my own to compose. What is your topic? Do you mean to address the Lords?"

"I mean to make a proposal of marriage. No doubt you can guess the object of my proposal." He winked.

Sir Rowan sat back. "Not Miss Neville?" he asked.

"Ah! I see that my sentiments are obvious to you and to the entire world. I am incapable of disguising my feelings. There is nothing I abhor so much as disguise, falsity, all that sort of thing. Furthermore, I do not *wish* to disguise my feelings."

The baronet bethought himself that a little disguise on his lordship's part would be most welcome.

Lord Mogglemere went on, "I believe the lady has an inkling of my attachment to her and will not be very much surprised by my offer. Of course, she will be obliged to feign surprise, for to appear to expect a gentleman's proposal is not at all the thing."

Little as he esteemed his lordship, Sir Rowan did not like to know that he, or any man, would soon find his most cherished hopes for the future suddenly blighted. He cast about for a gentle way to break the news and at last hit upon, "Permit me to advise caution. I believe you will not wish to speak to Miss Neville when you hear what I have to tell you."

"You are mistaken. I have made up my mind. My family hate the very idea of her, for she has scarcely any dowry, I am told, but I don't care for that. I mean to have her."

"You cannot have her. Miss Neville is engaged to me, sir."

Lord Mogglemere jumped up. "Damme. I thought you were after Miss Perrot. Now you go poaching after my deer. I say, a fellow ought to make up his mind."

"I regret it if you were misled. I am in love with Miss Neville and have always been."

"If I were a violent sort, I should call you out, sir."

"Call me out if you like, but it will not alter the fact that Miss Neville accepted me when I asked her to be my wife."

Mogglemere shifted about, frowning. "I don't understand it. Not once have I heard you remark on her sonnets. Not once, to my knowledge, have you demonstrated a proper solicitude for her muse. Not once have you pressed her to persevere in her poetry. And yet she accepts you. It is unaccountable."

Sir Rowan stood to face his companion. "If you are implying that I do not deserve her, I will agree with you. But let us shake hands and wish each other well, for I would not begrudge you your happiness were the situation reversed."

Pouting, Lord Mogglemere took a limp hold of Sir Rowan's fingers, then dropped them. "I do not need to wish you happy. With Miss Neville at your side, you cannot fail to be so the rest of your life. I, on the other hand, must content myself with hoping that you will learn some day to value her great gifts and do whatever is in your power to minister to them." Here he bowed his farewell and marched tragically from the coffeehouse.

CATHERINE STARED at Lord Byron, then laughed. "That is an absurd accusation," she said. "You must be bosky, sir."

Byron protested, "I've had no spirits these three hours. I am as clear-headed as you."

"If you were clear-headed, as you claim, you would not accuse Sir Rowan Heath of concocting such a poisonous piece. It is ridiculous."

Byron nodded. "Yes it is, rather. Sir Rowan is not generally given to directing his satire at literary objects. He has been kind enough to leave that sort of thing to me and to content himself with abusing those who have the power to retaliate. However, in this case, he has obviously made an exception."

"Why on earth should Sir Rowan write a review and sign Mr. Omsett's name to it?"

"I do not know, but he did."

"And why should he trouble himself with a book of poems? He is a political writer."

"I cannot answer that, either. I only know I have proof that he, not Tony Omsett, is the one who attacked Calvinia Nutter and her sister poets."

"What proof can you possibly have?"

"The best of proofs." Here he walked to a table where he had set a pile of journals and pamphlets. Opening one, he handed it to Catherine. With gravity, he sat down on a hard sofa and beckoned to her.

All at once, Catherine's confidence dissipated. Her fists tensed as she began to be aware of a sense of dread. Up to now, Byron's accusation appeared to her to have all the earmarks of jealousy. If he had guessed her feelings for Sir Rowan and his for her, he might not be above doing what mischief he could to separate them. That Lord Byron might have guessed her feelings would not surprise her. He was a penetrating, intuitive man, superior in this regard to almost any man she had ever known. One had only to read his poetry to know that he saw beneath appearances of every kind. Like his poems, his eyes bored through one's soul, it seemed, disinterring secrets. Her heart might be easily read by such a man, for she was not only innocent of wiles and pretence, but she did not much like them, either.

Now, however, he was offering proof, and his motive seemed not to be jealousy but a conviction of the truth. With reluctance, she approached the sofa and sat. Lord Byron did not attempt to seize her hand again. He only pointed his finger at a paragraph on the page he held open in front of him.

Catherine read an innocuous essay on Palladian architecture. The author indulged in rhapsodies on voluptuous friezes, scrolls of wood and plaster, and ornate medallions and shields. His delight in the Roman style was exceeded only by his delight in expressing delight. He was enchanted, he said, with scallop shells, gratified by acanthus scrolls over a fireplace, in raptures over stucco fruit and flowers. In short, nothing about the Palladian mode failed to send him into transports, and Catherine felt that if she continued to read these excesses of sentiment, she would soon be reduced to yawning.

"The author of this piece of excess is Mr. Anthony Omsett," Byron announced. So saying, he pointed to where the name was printed under the title in bold letters.

Seeing the name, Catherine felt a chill. The rhapsodic style of the essay was not at all the style of the piece in *The Gentleman's Review*.

At this juncture, Byron closed the journal and opened another. This time he presented an essay written in a very different vein. It was an attack on the English nation's adulation of Admiral Nelson, who even years after his death was still mentioned in ballads, on the stage and, most damaging of all, in Parliamentary speeches. The appearance of the naval hero's face in paintings and on plates, on crockery and ladies' frocks, on spoons and advertisements was a disgrace, the writer stated. Not only did it cheapen the very real accomplishments of one of the greatest Britons ever to sail the seas, but it also degraded the English character. Nothing was so detrimental to serious thought, railed the author, as the mindless and tasteless beatification of national heroes.

Catherine winced as she read, recognizing the scornful tone and knifelike wit. The author of this essay could easily have been the author of the attack on Calvinia Nutter. She did not need Byron to detail the many similarities of style, expression, opinion and tone, but he did so anyway, with painstaking precision. It gave him great satisfaction, she noted, to be able to point to the name printed under the title: Sir Rowan Heath, Bart. She shuddered.

If Catherine had any hope that Byron would be content with these two examples, she was mistaken, for he brought forth others, illustrating many times over the distinctly euphoric style of Mr. Omsett contrasted with the icy satire of Sir Rowan.

"Enough," Catherine said at last. "I have seen the evidence. It cannot be refuted."

Repressing his glee, Byron said mournfully, "I regret having to be the bearer of the truth. I know it shocks and pains you."

Rising from the sofa, she turned on him. "If you regret it, then why did you do it?"

He set his pile of evidence to one side and rose. "I am only the messenger, dear lady. I am not the perpetrator."

Catherine looked away, afraid that he would see the tears start. "I apologize," she said unsteadily. "Of course, you are blameless."

Byron was taken aback. For the first time in his life, he had heard someone pronounce him blameless. He liked the sensation, not to mention the novelty. He must remind himself to be blameless more often, he thought.

Quietly, Catherine said, "You will understand, sir, if I beg you to leave me now."

Here he fixed her with his dark eyes and said, "I cannot leave you in such a state."

"Then *I* will leave *you*," she said, making for the door.

"Wait!" he cried. Striding to her, he lifted her hand to his lips. "Do not think," he said in a near whisper, "that I intend to leave you disappointed and disillusioned. You must know that I am your unwavering friend. Whatever I can do to bring you solace, you have only to name it and it shall be done. I shall spare no effort. Mayhap, I shall write you a poem."

With an effort at patience, Catherine replied, "You have already promised me a poem. You promised it to me last night, but I do not see it anywhere. All I have seen are those vile papers of yours."

He clapped his hand to his forehead. "Gad, in the rush of investigating the true authorship of the review, I forgot to write the poem. I vow, I shall get right to it."

It struck Catherine now that she had not thanked Byron for telling her the truth. She had spoken irritably to him, even though he deserved better from her. Therefore, she said, "I must apologize again, my lord. It seems I cannot help letting you bear the brunt of my distress. I did not mean to snap at you, and you need not bother about the poem."

"You cannot tell a poet not to bother about a poem, madam. You may as well tell Prinny not to dine out but to content himself at home with a bowl of porridge. I shall bring you the poem I promised this evening."

"I am engaged for the theatre this evening," she said unhappily. She regretted having promised Lord Perrot she would go to Covent Garden with the family. There was nothing so repellent to her just now as the thought of having to go into Society. She felt a sudden dryness block her throat. Not knowing how long she would be able to maintain an air of calm, she moved to open the door.

He put his hand over hers, stopping her. She pulled her hand away and found herself trapped by his nearness.

"In that case, I shall come to your box at the theatre," he whispered. "Meanwhile, *adieu*." Here his lips came close to her ear as he opened the door for her, allowing her to escape.

WHEN HE CALLED in Curzon Street, Sir Rowan was surprised to find Catherine denied to him. He felt certain that no matter how unwell she felt, she would consent to see him, especially after what had passed between them the night before. That she kept to her room could mean only one thing—her indisposition was grave. The idea agitated him sharply. He enquired of the butler whether Miss Neville had fever and whether the doctor had been sent for.

Before the servant could answer, Miss Perrot interrupted. "Sir Rowan," she addressed him loftily. "I would have a word with you, if you please."

He stepped with her into the parlour, hoping to glean news of Catherine's condition.

He had no opportunity to do so, however, because Miss Perrot said, as soon as they had seated themselves, "I wish to say that I harbour no rancour against you, sir."

The baronet's left eyebrow rose as he absorbed this curious announcement.

Philippa continued, "I speak of this grievous subject 'more in sorrow than in anger,' as Shakespeare says. You do not object to my alluding to Shakespeare, I hope."

"Object? I take heart from hearing him quoted. It is what every scribbler aspires to."

"There are those who are of the opinion that you hate quotations."

Sir Rowan wondered who could have been misrepresenting him, but he knew that if he enquired further, he would be in for more Shakespeare. Besides, he wished to hear news of Catherine.

"My intention in seeking this private interview is to tell you that I do not blame you. If blame is to be laid anywhere, it is at the door of scheming country girls who will stoop to vile arts in their pursuit of an advantageous match."

Out of patience now, Sir Rowan interjected, "My dear Miss Perrot, I wish to speak of Miss Neville."

Philippa coloured and said coldly, "Naturally, I wish you very happy, but I think it highly unlikely you will be."

"Miss Neville was unwell when I asked for her. Can you tell me how she does?"

"She does well enough to accompany us to the theatre tonight. I am sure I should not care if she stayed at home, but my father will have her come."

Sir Rowan was baffled. "This is very strange," he said. "You say Miss Neville means to go to the theatre, but I am told she is too ill to receive today."

With a shrug, Philippa replied, "Mayhap the lady is capricious. I should not be in the least surprised if she were sick to dying one moment and ready to walk the length of Hyde Park the next."

He knew Catherine too well to believe her capricious. Even if she were, the warmth of her kisses was proof that she would make an exception in his case. No, there was something else afoot here, and he began to suspect what it was. Only one thing could account for her behaviour: she had found out. Somehow, she had learned the truth before he had been able to tell her.

Suddenly he felt ill. How much damage would his absurd, careless boast about writing a review inflict before it was done? How many times would Catherine be subjected to the painful consequences of his error? How many times would he be obliged to imagine her pain and feel it himself?

Before Miss Perrot could embark on another extract, elegant or otherwise, he bade her farewell and hurried from the house. He had much to do if he was going to be in Covent Garden that evening.

LORD PERROT ESCORTED the four ladies of his household to the Theatre Royal at Covent Garden through the Bow Street entrance under the portico. From there, the party climbed the grand staircase which led to an anteroom. They were permitted four seconds in which to admire a fine figure of Shakespeare, and were then herded by his lordship toward the lower tier of boxes. After settling themselves in chairs, they scanned the theatre to see who amongst their acquaintance would nod and wave to them.

Patrons of the theatre were charged an outrageous sum for tickets, Lord Perrot complained. Kemble would have done better not to rebuild the place after the fire, but to let it lie in ruins until sufficient funds were raised. This business of rebuilding on a grand scale, without any thought to economy, would come to no good. The rabble were grumbling and had already rioted in anger against the price. If he were not a gentleman and a Tory, he would have rioted himself.

Lady Perrot paid no mind to her husband; nor did his daughters hear a word he said. Only Catherine listened, and she did so not out of any great curiosity to know how the restoration of the great hall had been accomplished, but because she felt numb.

She had been unable to bring herself to see Sir Rowan when he had called earlier in Curzon Street. Obeying her instructions, the butler had recited a short speech: "Miss Neville begs to say that she is unwell this afternoon." Catherine had hidden herself on an upper landing of the staircase in order to hear the speech delivered. Sir Rowan appeared to take the news without perturbation, for which she hardly knew whether to be grateful or grieved.

She had not wished to join the family in the outing to Covent Garden. Her intention was to plead a headache and to cry her eyes out in private. Although in general she loved a play and especially a comedy, she was not disposed to laugh at the moment. Moreover, she wished to avoid the company of Lady Perrot and Philippa, who were not speaking to her.

But Lord Perrot would not let her beg off. "A play will cheer you," he said, "and by the look on your charming face, you do want some cheering. Grimaldi will do the job. You cannot frown while Grimaldi is clowning." Thankful for his lordship's kind solicitude, Catherine had agreed to make one of the party.

The snubs of her ladyship and Miss Perrot distressed her, as she had known they would, but his lordship did not allow her many minutes for distress. As they sat in their box, he admired the theatre, and because he despaired of interesting his wife or daughters in his observations on it, he pointed out to Catherine sundry features of the Ionic architecture, the unusual form of the cut-glass chandeliers, and the gold-fretted flowers fronting each box. The expense of rebuilding might be a perfect scandal, his lordship assured her, but there was no gain-saying that the end result was entirely splendid.

As she listened, Catherine looked at the faces in the other boxes. For a time, she was able to persuade herself that she sought the face of Lord Byron, who had threat-ened to put in an appearance merely in order to deliver her poem. She told herself that it was the most natural thing in the world to be curious to see whether he would make good on his promise. But she could not deceive herself for long. She was searching for the face of Sir Rowan, and if she saw him, and if he saw her, she did not know how she would contrive to meet his eyes.

Lord Byron entered Lord Perrot's box and drew up a chair just behind Catherine's right shoulder. Lord Per-rot was glad to have the company of the young gentle-man, for since he had extended his invitation to Miss Neville, his wife and daughter had declined to speak to him or look at him, and he required a diversion. Byron was nothing if not diverting. He flirted with Daphne, chucking her under her chin when her mama was not looking, and he listened reverently as Philippa enun-ciated excerpts from *English Bards and Scots Reviewers*, a recitation delivered with such solemnity that the poet wondered how he had contrived to write such a dreary poem. He conversed with Lord Perrot on politics, con-fessed he had given a speech in the House of Lords and asked whether it was true his lordship kept the best store of port in all of England, a charge which Lord Perrot vigorously denied.

At last, Byron unfolded a poem which, he announced
to the family, he had written for Miss Neville. The lyric
had its faults, he would not deny it, but considering that
he had had only a few hours in which to compose it, he
thought it was rather fine. He begged their indulgence,
and with his brooding brown eyes flashing and his handsome countenance brilliant with animation, he read:

> I saw thee weep—the big bright tear
> Came o'er that eye of blue;
> And then, methought, it did appear
> A violet dropping dew:
> I saw thee smile—the sapphire's blaze
> Beside thee ceascd to shine;
> It could not match the living rays
> That filled that glance of thine.

"It rhymes pleasantly enough," Daphne observed.

Philippa, quite moved by the lyric, exclaimed, "What
excellent images! The 'violet dropping dew'! It is most
affecting. One might almost weep."

Catherine said nothing, but only stared at a box directly opposite. She saw Sir Rowan standing half in
shadow by the drape. He was watching her. She had the
sense that he had been watching her for some time. He
wore a look of such gravity that she knew at once how
things stood. He knew she knew.

The knowledge gave her some relief. As long as they
both knew the truth, there would be no need for pretence, no need for her to upbraid him with the facts, no
need to tell him that their engagement was broken. It was
all over.

But he looked at her with such steadfastness, such seriousness, that she could feel the intensity of his eyes,

even at that distance. The look did not escape the notice of several of the other theatre patrons. They glanced from him to her and back again, grinning, as if to see what would come from such looks. Soon, half the audience was watching them look at each other—all except the gallery, which hooted and howled for the performance to start. At last, their looks caught the attention of the Perrots. Philippa and her ladyship evinced disgust at the display. Daphne remarked, "With such looks, I declare Sir Rowan will set the place on fire again." And Lord Byron, seeing that everyone was occupied with watching Sir Rowan as he watched Miss Neville, took the opportunity to plant a kiss on that young lady's bare shoulder.

CHAPTER NINE

THE LIGHTS DIMMED, calling everyone's attention to the stage. Under cover of darkness, Catherine turned to Byron. "Writing a poem for me does not give you the right to take liberties, sir," she said in a low but unmistakable tone of displeasure. She did not wait for his apology, but rose, brushed quickly past him, and left the box.

In the vast hall, lighted by enormous chandeliers and adorned with life-size scenes from *Love's Labour's Lost* and *The Tragedy of Romeo and Juliet*, Catherine had the sudden sense of being overwhelmed. She leaned against a pillar at the top of an elaborate staircase and fanned herself. It had been ill-mannered of her to leave the box. She ought to return before the others came after her. Yet it was better to stand in the hall feeling dwarfed and insignificant than to hit Byron in the face, as she had been sorely tempted to do. He was a fine-featured gentleman, and she could not be insensible to his attractions, but his kiss on her shoulder had caused her teeth to grind. She could not help wondering if Sir Rowan had seen it.

No sooner had the thought entered her mind than Sir Rowan himself came round a corner and stopped at the bottom of the staircase. Fixing his eyes on her, he ascended the stairs at a slow, deliberate pace. He walked with dignity, the more so, it seemed, because his expression was severe. She thought of escaping to the safety of the Perrot box, but because she could not do what she knew to be cowardly, she collected her emotions and waited.

As she watched him mount the stairs, she was startled to see that he looked the same as he had always looked. She had expected him now to wear a harsh face, a penetrating gleam, a sardonic smile, for he was not the same man she had fallen in love with. The man she loved was possessed of understanding, humour and a depth of feeling. He was a man who had taken pity on poor, terrified Miss Perrot, a man who laughed at himself as well as the world, a man who blamed himself for his sister's tragic fate. But this other man—the one who had written the review—was a stranger, a man who hid beneath his fine-looking exterior a fund of cruelty, a man who confused and frightened her. Nothing could reconcile this stranger with the man she loved.

The irony was that he had warned her. He had told her on more than one occasion that he was a careless fellow. She ought to have believed him.

When he reached her, he said simply, "I make no attempt to excuse myself to you, Catherine, but I wish you to know that I meant to tell you everything myself. That was my purpose in coming to Curzon Street this afternoon."

She bowed her head slightly. "Of course, I have no way of knowing whether you are telling the truth. But your visit would have been superfluous. By the time it was made, I had already learned the truth."

"I guessed as much. I would have come earlier, but I was required to think what to say to you."

"Yes, I would imagine you wished to choose your words carefully this time. You would not wish to employ the same style of composition you used for *The Gentleman's Review*. However, it does not matter now."

"If our engagement does not matter, then I suppose you are right." He tried to read her eyes, but she kept them averted.

With an effort, she said, "There can be no engagement."

"I know you cannot overlook my carelessness in writing such a piece. I thought you might be able to forgive it."

"It is not a question of forgiving, I assure you."

"But surely you are not resentful on account of your poems. I know you too well to think you are rancorous toward unfavourable reviewers, just or unjust."

"I do not dispute your freedom—your licence—to say anything you like about my poems. The satire may wound momentarily, but the feeling cannot last. What does last is the suspicion of what prompts such a review."

He stepped close to her. "I was careless, I own. I knew it almost at once and took another review, a just one, to Tony the very next day. He promised to use it in place of the original, only he never got round to making the substitution. You may ask him if you cannot believe me."

Looking at her gloved hands, she said, "I do believe you. You may be careless, but I have not known you to lie."

"Then say you forgive me."

"I do. I do forgive you."

"And that you love me as much as I love you."

Here she turned her back to him. Seeing her pale skin against her white pearl-seeded gown, he came near, taking her by the arms, hoping that she would lean back so that he might bury his face in her hair.

She remained rigid, however. At last she said, "I do. I do love you." Then, turning to face him, she said, "But I cannot marry you."

"Catherine, you say you love me and yet you are prepared to toss everything away. I don't dismiss what I did. Nor do I ask you to dismiss it, but is it worth ending what is between us? I cannot believe you will not feel the consequences of a break as much as I."

She bowed her head. "Yes, I will feel it, and every bit as much as you. But that is nothing to what I would feel if we married and, soon afterward, you grew careless in your manner toward me. Oh, I know that now you think you cannot live without me and that you will always treasure me, but you and I are both too many years out of the schoolroom to imagine that there will not be changes."

"Very well. Let us say there will be changes. Why should they cause you to cry off now, when last night you were prepared to accept me?"

"Because I did not see last night what I see this night— that you are two men. One I could marry; the other would wound me with his cruelty. I am not able to love you both."

Inhaling, he said, "My God, I've made you afraid of me."

"I have seen what savage language you are capable of. To become your wife, I should have to countenance it, ignore it or laugh at it with you. I know myself too well to imagine I am capable of doing any of these things. I should wither in such a marriage."

"You are wrong, my dearest Catherine. The bleak picture you paint is wholly inaccurate. But I will not try to win you with arguments, for I see that you do not trust me and no mere words can change that. As to our engagement, you have ended it and I shall make no attempt to persuade you to do otherwise. I will not see you spend every hour in my company wondering what I am really thinking, living in dread that I am about to subject you to a verbal assault. I won't ask you to live that sort of life, though I know in my heart that you would never have anything to fear from me.''

Her eyes and throat were too full to permit her to answer.

Seeing the emotion on her face, he could not help reaching for her. She did not resist as he pulled her to him, but after desperately kissing him once, she broke free and returned to the box at a run.

Sir Rowan took a breath and thoughtfully descended the stairs. During his life as a gentleman of the Town, he had always scorned the vaunted power of the pen. It seemed to him that the press scribbled, the novelists scribbled, the poets scribbled, the pamphleteers scribbled, and all to little avail. He had heard it said that the writings of Tom Paine had fomented the revolution in the American colonies and that it had been Voltaire and Rousseau who had done the business in France, but he had not believed it. His years as a writer of political essays had persuaded him that revolutions came about because of greed, because the middle classes wished to wield the political power that enhanced their profits, because the lower classes saw an opportunity to take what they envied in others instead of working for it, and because the aristocracy were too selfish and effete to reform either the laws or their extravagant ways. He could not believe in the power of the pen because nothing he had ever written about a politician had succeeded in improving the fellow's conduct. A member of Parliament might take the trouble to hire a pair of ruffians to waylay him in a London alley at night, but the fellow would not go so far as to cease practicing nepotism, taking brides or profiting privately at the government's expense.

Now, however, seeing how a trivial review he had written had turned his life upside down, he was forced to allow that he owed the written word more regard than he had accorded it in the past. What he had written in a careless moment had given pain to the single person in the world he most wished to make happy. He felt as though he had gone in an instant from acting the hero in a comedy to portraying the villain in a tragedy. Catherine was afraid of him. She did not trust him to be tender of her feelings.

He had said he would not attempt to argue her out of her fears, and he meant to keep that promise. What he had in view was more than arguments; it was example. Whenever they should meet in future—and he meant to see to it that they met often—he would show her what sort of behaviour she might expect from him. She would learn to trust him. She would come to see that a man may have a public persona, which allows him to view the world with cynicism and still be gentle in private. Thus resolved, he did not return to his box, but walked through the high, imposing, empty anterooms until he found his way out of the theatre.

As SHE RESUMED her seat in the box, Catherine could not rid her mind of one thought. It was a ridiculous thought, she told herself, and one not at all to the purpose. Ridiculous as it was, however, she could not help dwelling on the fact that Sir Rowan had not mentioned Lord Byron's kiss. She was safe in concluding, she told herself, that he had not seen it. Not for the world would she have him see another man kiss her.

Of course, they were no longer to be married. Of course, she need not concern herself with the agitation he must feel at the knowledge that he had a rival. Still, she could not disregard his feelings. He might be cruel, satiric and callous when he chose, but she wished to spare him pain.

Grimaldi, who bounced abut the stage in his clown's dress, was endeavouring to feed a frog. The actor who played the frog hopped merrily about, upsetting Grimaldi's plate of food as well as his balance, so that he rolled like a motley ball before the footlights. This piece of business provoked an uproar of laughter in the theatre, with as much hilarity descending from the boxes as rising from the one-shilling seats in the gallery. None of the foolery won Catherine from her thoughts, however.

She did not blame Sir Rowan for being what he was. They lived, after all, in a satirical age. Very little was to be taken seriously. Everything was inconsequential, amusing, unimpassioned. One saw it in the clothing, which was worn in pale, subdued colours; in the buildings, which were designed along classic lines of restraint, in the drawings and etchings, which captured pleasant, mild landscapes. Gentlemen who regarded the world with insouciance were the ideal. Indeed, Sir Rowan's carelessness was the very thing that the age admired in him. To say the truth, she herself had found it fascinating.

But she could not pretend that words did not hurt her, that a husband's carelessness of manner or feeling would not pain her. And so she had done the only thing she could do: she had broken with him.

As she wiped tears from her cheeks, she suddenly felt someone fold a paper into her hand. Looking around, she saw Byron. He regarded her seriously and, it seemed to her, sympathetically. He neither winked nor moved to touch her. With his eyes, he indicated the paper he had given her. Opening it, she read by the dim light, the words, "I saw thee weep—the big bright tear," and she could read no further.

EARLY THE FOLLOWING MORNING, Catherine appeared in the breakfast parlour dressed for travelling. When the ladies glanced up from their sausage and toast, she announced that she was setting forth for The Priors that very hour. Lady Perrot was not sorry to see her troublesome guest depart, but could not help saying, "But how will you get your things packed in time? You cannot travel without your dresses and jewels and such."

"I have been awake all night with the servant," Catherine replied, "and we have contrived to get everything packed."

Vexed, Daphne declared, "You cannot have considered my feelings in leaving so hastily, for, without your protection, I shall be left with Philippa, who will prose at me from dawn to dusk."

Catherine smiled. "I thank you for your kindness to me," she said. "And now I must be off."

"Wait!" Daphne cried. "Mama, Philippa, you will not let her go, will you? Philippa, say something. You always have something to say."

Every eye turned on Philippa then, who at last intoned, *"Omnis festinatio est a Diabolo."*

Daphne rolled her eyes to heaven. "Say it in English, you toad!"

Loftily, Philippa translated, "All haste is from the devil." She then rose from her chair and glided from the room without vouchsafing Miss Neville a farewell.

Stung, Catherine turned on her heel and went out to the hall. Daphne followed close behind. Spying her father there on his way out the door, she cried to him, "Papa, do not let Miss Neville go. She is the only amusing companion in the house. I shall perish with boredom if she is permitted to go."

Lord Perrot gaped. "You are leaving us, Miss Neville?"

"I ought to have left sooner, my lord. I am wanted at The Priors. My sister is with child, you see."

Daphne cried, "I do not see what you can do if she is with child. The damage has already been done. And besides, you cannot possibly leave London before the end of the Season. No one ever heard of such a thing."

Catherine said nothing, but remained firm.

"Stop her, Papa," Daphne begged her father.

He whispered to his daughter, "I had better keep mum, my dear. Your mother and your sister are already angry at me for taking the young lady to Covent Garden last night. I do not know what they will do if I persuade her to stay."

Daphne pouted. "Very well. I shall absolutely die in this house with no one to laugh with and Philippa raining Latin on my head." Here she wagged a finger and levelled an ominous look at Lord Perrot. "I shall be perfectly miserable, and it will all be your fault!" she sobbed. On that, she ran to her chamber, forgetting to take leave of the young woman whose presence was apparently so necessary to her health and happiness.

His lordship sighed. He supposed it would be some time before he found himself in the good graces of all three of the females in his household at the same time. He therefore turned his attention to Miss Neville. "Do you mean to travel by post?"

"Why, yes."

"That you shall not. If you must leave us, so be it, though I vow I shall miss you as much as Daphne will. You are a sensible, cheerful young miss, and not as disagreeable as the generality of females. But my brother-in-law will have my hide if I let you go by post. You shall take my carriage."

Catherine expressed her gratitude, and sat down in the hall, still wearing her pelisse and hat, while his lordship summoned a servant to ready the carriage. When all had been arranged and Lord Perrot had handed Miss Neville inside the conveyance, he waved her goodbye with considerable regret. So low did he feel that he considered he owed it to himself to uncork another bottle of his port, and to steal away into a closet under the stairs in order to savour it.

LATER IN THE DAY, Lord Mogglemere called. About the same time, Byron called. Then another knock was sounded and the caller proved to be Sir Rowan. Each of the gentlemen in turn asked the butler to announce him to Miss Neville, and each was told that the young lady had gone to Kent.

"She is gone!" exclaimed Mogglemere to the other two. "But I do not understand her leaving London." Turning to look at Sir Rowan, he continued, "I had heard she was to be married."

"That is undoubtedly why she fled," Byron remarked.

"Oh, but this is unaccountable," Mogglemere cried.

"We shall have to find poor Mogglemere another poetess to dote on, eh, Heath?" Byron remarked to Sir Rowan.

The baronet contrived to smile at the sally. "I daresay we forget our manners, gentlemen," he said. "Even if

Miss Neville has gone, it behooves us, I think, to pay a call on the other ladies of the house.''

"Do we have to?'' Mogglemere asked.

Amazed at Sir Rowan's suggestion, Byron enquired, "When did you become such a model of politeness?''

Blithely, the baronet ignored both questions and said, "If the ladies hear we called but did not ask for them, they will feel slighted.''

"And what if they do?'' Byron asked.

"I say,'' Mogglemere added, "Byron is right. I have had far too much distressing news of Miss Neville these last two days to face the ladies of the house.''

"Then I shall bid you good day, friends, and pay the call myself.'' Here he asked the servant to announce him to Lady Perrot.

In half a minute the footman returned to say that the ladies were within and would be pleased to see Sir Rowan. As the baronet followed the servant to the blue sitting room, the other two gentlemen made their escape.

SIR ROWAN WAS RESOLVED to conduct himself as though Catherine were in the room, observing his manners and air. Consequently, he bestirred himself to consider the sensibilities of the three ladies who sat before him, arranged picturesquely on a ring of Chippendale chairs in the Gothic style. That these ladies *had* sensibilities to be considered he would have to take on faith. The thought had never entered his mind before.

Although the conversation dwelt on inconsequentials, he noticed for the first time that Lady Perrot appeared haggard beneath her rouge. The ordeal of trying to marry off two dreadful daughters had taken its toll on her disposition. Fretful, complaining, hypochondriacal, she could barely speak to him in a civil tone.

Miss Perrot also presented a new aspect to him as he observed her from a new perspective. He saw that she was a tense young woman who kept herself in check. All her philosophy, he suspected, had been martialled to enable her to assume a posture of tranquillity. She had succeeded in affixing a smile to her face, but she spoke not a word to him for the entire duration of his visit.

In contrast, Daphne welcomed his entrance with gratitude. She spoke no more sensibly or kindly than she had before Sir Rowan had resolved to mend his manners. Nevertheless, she kept up a flow of chatter that masked the reserve of the other two.

Assuming that the general want of spirits could be attributed to Miss Neville's departure, he began to regard the ladies with considerable gentleness. He himself regretted her departure more than he could say, and so he could well understand their lowness in the face of it. He refrained from alluding to the loss of Miss Neville's company, thinking that it might be of greater benefit to them all to suggest a diversion. To that end, he mentioned a public assembly at Hampstead and offered to procure tickets for them all. And though it cost him a moment's pang, he ventured to include Mogglemere and Byron in the scheme.

"Will you invite Mr. Omsett?" Daphne pleaded. "I am sure he must be an excellent dancer."

"If it will make you smile, and do something toward alleviating the frowns on the other charming faces in the room, I shall certainly invite Mr. Omsett."

At this flattery, Lady Perrot and Philippa began to soften. Sir Rowan, when he exerted himself to be polite, was irresistible, and so they could not help but be won over. Daphne beamed with satisfaction, and the scheme was approved all round.

As he left them, Sir Rowan congratulated himself on his exemplary manners. Had Catherine witnessed them, she would have been forced to confess that he was capable of being a very model of gallantry. But the real test would be to see if he could sustain such efforts beyond a visit lasting a mere quarter hour.

Another question—a more crucial one by far—was how he was to put himself in Catherine's way now that she had gone from London. His only hope was that his attentions to the Perrot ladies would end by keeping him apprised of the latest news of her, so that if she did return to Town, he would be the first to hear of it.

The likelihood of her returning, however, was miniscule. The Season was nearly over. The exodus to the country would soon begin. And it would be months before he would set eyes on that delicate honey-gold hair, those blue eyes, and the warm, rosy expression. She would forget him by then, while he would still see her whenever he closed his eyes at night, and whenever he opened them in the morning.

CHAPTER TEN

SIR ROWAN'S VISIT, following as it did so closely upon Miss Neville's departure, could not fail to cause remark among the Perrot ladies. It was Daphne who stated aloud what they had all found amazing, namely, that not once had the gentleman mentioned Miss Neville's name, let alone her sudden decision to leave London.

"Odd behaviour in a gentleman who is supposed to be engaged to a lady, I daresay," Lady Perrot observed.

"Odd?" cried Daphne. "Why, it is unfeeling in the extreme. But it does not surprise me. Gentlemen have no heart nowadays. You have only to look at Mr. Omsett by way of illustration. I'm sure he has not called these three days."

Philippa's eyes blinked as an idea took possession of her mind and would not let go. "Perhaps the behaviour is not as odd as it first appears," she said darkly. "Perhaps Sir Rowan said nothing for the very good reason that he had nothing to say." Here she nodded her head sagely.

Daphne refused to let her sister's innuendo pique her curiosity. "He not only failed to speak Miss Neville's name," she went on, "but he appeared not at all put out by her absence. I vow, his calling upon us was prodigiously civil, but I did not expect it."

"Perhaps there is a reason for his not being put out," Philippa said. "Perhaps there is excellent reason for his prodigious civility."

Popping out of her chair, Daphne shrieked, "Spare us these infernal 'perhapses' and that smug look of yours, unless you mean to tell us what in the name of mercy you are rattling on about!"

Philippa smiled at her sister and said, "Perhaps I shall tell you."

Throwing up her hands, Daphne sank into her chair, while her mother said, "Philippa, my dear, I have the vilest headache. If you say anything now that is even remotely connected to Shakespeare or his set, I shall disinherit you. Now, say what you have to say and be done with it."

"What I have to say is this, Mama—perhaps there was never any engagement between Sir Rowan and Miss Neville. Perhaps that explains his tranquillity in our presence just now and his not noticing Miss Neville's absence. Perhaps the engagement was merely an invention of Miss Neville's. Poets are skilled at invention, you know. They could not see tears in a drop of dew if they were not skilful inventors."

"I have warned you, Philippa," said her mother. "Not a single epigram."

"There was not the hint of an epigram in anything I said, Mama. I take my oath."

"Very well, you may continue."

"Perhaps Miss Neville suddenly flew to Kent because she had discovered there was no engagement. Perhaps she had read too much into Sir Rowan's attentions, more than was there, and then learned the truth of the matter."

"I believe you have smoked it!" her ladyship declared.

"It is a rational explanation," Daphne agreed. "After all, the very same thing happened to Philippa. She read too much into Sir Rowan's attentions, and then got her comeuppance."

"Daphne, you will not speak of that," instructed her mother. "If Miss Neville has left London in mortification, then perhaps Philippa still has a chance of catching the gentleman. Indeed, I begin to feel that there cannot have been any engagement between them, that it was Miss Neville's fabrication from the outset, and that Philippa must dance with Sir Rowan at Hampstead."

Smiling as she had not smiled in days, Philippa vowed that she would dance with the baronet. She made a second vow as well—that she would permit to issue from her lips any salient quotations that came into her head. She would not withhold a single extract that might enlighten and edify the man whose heart she planned to capture, and she would free herself from the narrow-minded strictures of her mother so as to pour out to her lover the full store of wisdom in her heart. But this vow she made only to herself. She did not wish to hear her mother's and sister's warnings on the subject, any more than she wished to spend the rest of her life with a husband who expected her to repress her foremost talent.

THE COUNTESS OF TICEHURST, formerly Miss Anne Neville, saw that something was amiss the instant her sister stepped from the carriage. She was not alarmed at having received no warning of Catherine's arrival. Nor was she unduly distressed at the evident haste with which her sister had packed. What struck her as singularly troublesome was the manner and air her sister wore, the man-

ner and air she had worn of old, before celebrity had
drawn her into Society, before she had given up her safe
position as an unnoticed observer instead of a partici-
pant. Anne knew her sister well, and despite their long
months of separation, she could see at once that in coming to The Priors, Catherine had effectively withdrawn
from the world.

The sisters embraced in the small vestibule at the entrance to the modern wing of the house. It was a bright
room, redolent of the colour and fragrance of the first
blossoms of summer. The effect was to make Catherine
feel at home, and if her sister's embrace had not assured
her of her welcome, her brother-in-law's warm greeting
could leave no doubt of it.

The ladies bustled to the very best guest bedroom, one
which Queen Charlotte herself had graced with her presence one stormy night many years earlier, and one which
boasted a southeast aspect, so that it attracted sunshine
for much of the day. Exhausted, Catherine stretched
herself out on the soft quilt which covered the bed, while
Anne prepared to cross-examine her.

"Why did you not tell me you were coming?"

Catherine sighed. "I hope you do not mind the surprise. I have been wanting to come these many weeks, but
allowed myself to be persuaded to stay in Town. Now I
have gratified myself by doing as I wished."

"But why now, when it is so close to the end of the
Season? I'm afraid there is little to entertain a celebrated
poet in this quiet part of the country."

"That is just what I hoped."

Anne frowned at this sentiment. Sitting down in a
sturdy cow-hocked chair, she shook her head. "My dear
Cathy, you cannot fool me. You have that old mousy

look about the eyes. You have not come to visit me; you've come to escape from London.''

Catherine smiled. ''You understand me too well for me to pretend otherwise. However—'' and here she grew serious ''—I am not prepared to speak of what brings me here so unexpectedly. I know you will not press me before I am ready.''

Anne's first impulse was to press her sister and press her hard until she had unfolded the whole tale of her flight. However, she refrained. She would not distress her, at least not on the first day of her visit. There would be time enough, when Catherine was settled, to conduct an interrogation. In the meantime, she was at liberty to indulge in a conjecture or two.

SHE DID SO INDULGE an hour later, when she sat in a cosy parlour with her lord and his dogs. While she stitched at a piece of fine work, he dozed over his newspaper, snoring in tune with the animals.

''Binky,'' she said, causing him to wake with a start, ''what is your opinion of this visit of my sister's?''

He blinked, the better to concentrate on forming a reply. Then he said, ''My opinion is that she is most welcome.''

Making a noise of disgust, Anne said, ''What is that to the purpose, my love? What I am asking is what you make of it?''

''Oh, you wish to know what I make of it? What I make of it is, well, it's difficult to say, isn't it? I mean, she will certainly be a delightful addition to our small family party here, and you must be grateful for her companionship, my love.''

''Well,'' she persevered, ''what do you make of it, my love?''

Here he tensed again. Then he hit on the expedient of answering, "Well, what do *you* make of it, my love?"

"I shall tell you what I make of it. She has quarrelled with your sister and the harridan has sent Cathy flying to us, poor child."

The angry tone in his wife's voice gave his lordship pause. As Earl of Ticehurst, he was master of extensive lands and landlord to a multitude of tenants. He acted as magistrate in the county and had kept the district well supplied with food, despite the depleted national stores caused by the war. Nevertheless, the earl deferred to his wife in all matters not directly related to the dispensation of food or justice. Hence, he thought ponderously before observing, "Sally has been known to be quarrelsome."

"Quarrelsome! Why, she never wanted Cathy to begin with. I knew, as soon as she asked you for money to chaperon my sister in Town, that she would find a way to make the poor girl's life a perfect misery."

"If it is true that Sally has driven Catherine away, my love, then I am very glad she thought to come to us."

"What do you mean 'if it is true'?"

Here his lordship slunk into his chair and fixed his eyes on an item in the newspaper. "Well, I don't suppose I mean much of anything by it."

"You said 'if it is true.' Surely you must mean something."

"If you say I mean something, my love, then I am sure you are right."

Anne threw her embroidery aside, crying, "You are not telling me what you think, Binky. You are withholding something from me. Do not spare me, my love. However bad it might be, I wish to hear it."

Obliged to supply something for his wife to hear, the earl bit his lip and furrowed his brow. At last he said, "We do not actually know that Sally and your sister have quarrelled, do we?"

"That is true, I suppose. I thought it a natural conclusion, but I have no actual proof. Cathy will not tell me what drove her from London."

"Precisely."

"I see what you are thinking!" Anne exclaimed. "You are suggesting that because we have no proof of a quarrel, there may be some other reason why Cathy has fled to us."

"Oh, that is excellent, my love."

"But if a quarrel is not the reason, then what is?"

His lordship was conscious that his wife was expecting another answer, and so once again he endeavoured to put his mind to work. Impatiently, the lady waited until her lord ventured to say, "Mayhap she's broken her heart."

Here Anne rose from her chair. "Good heavens, Binky, I believe that's it."

"It is?"

"I ought to have thought of it myself."

"Well, as long as one of us thought of it, my love."

"Some scoundrel, some villain has jilted my poor Cathy."

"I am glad you are pleased with that answer, my love. And now I am off to the Meadows with the steward." He rose and went to the door. "If you have need of any further answers, you will have to wait until this evening. If you write down the questions, you will not forget them."

"Binky," Anne said with a smile. He turned and waited while she approached. "You are a clever thing, you are, hitting on the answer while I flew into a tizzy over your sister.''

He beamed. She stood on tiptoe to peck him on the cheek. ''There,'' she said. ''You have your reward. Now go and make the crops grow, you wise old thing, you.''

Grateful to have escaped so brilliantly, he marched contentedly out the door, while his lady seated herself again, took up her work once more and considered what might be the best means of mending her sister's broken heart.

THE ASSEMBLY at Hampstead was a most pleasurable outing. Daphne had the pleasure of dancing two dances with Tony Omsett. Tony Omsett had the pleasure of being flirted with by a very brazen Daphne Perrot. Lady Perrot had the pleasure of seeing her eldest daughter dance with Sir Rowan Heath. Philippa had the pleasure of reciting a speech to the baronet. And Sir Rowan had the pleasure of putting his plan into action.

As he had known the Earl of Ticehurst many years, Sir Rowan might pay a visit to The Priors on no other pretext than that of seeing his old friend. However, if Catherine guessed that he had come purely on her account, his arrival might cause her to bolt. The best way to avoid such a calamity, he saw, was to appear to be visiting Miss Perrot, at the invitation of her mother.

Consequently, he danced with Miss Perrot and listened with hardly a glazed eye to her recitation of Fordyce's sermon on penitence. Next he escorted the young woman to a pillar by which the mother sat and engaged them both in amiable conversation, saying, ''I suppose you mean to go into the country soon.''

The ladies confessed that they found country life tiresome.

"I wish your father had thought to purchase an estate in the south," her ladyship complained to Philippa. "I suppose he will cart us off to Scotland."

"Scotland is of all places the most dreary," Philippa declared.

"Your brother lives in the south, does he not?" the baronet enquired, as though the idea had only just occurred to him.

"Yes," her ladyship said with a sigh.

"Well, you may go to him in Kent if you do not like Scotland," he said.

Her ladyship did not look very sanguine at this prospect. "I do not know whether my brother will invite me," she said. "The countess is with child."

"All the more reason to have good society near at hand." He smiled in a way that won a smile from the ladies.

"I suppose my brother might invite us," Lady Perrot said without much conviction.

Sir Rowan replied, "A sister does not need an invitation, I trust. A sister may go at any time to see a brother to whom she is warmly attached by sentiment as well as by blood." He hoped this speech was as polite as it was insincere.

"Sir Rowan is right," Philippa said. " 'The voice of a brother's blood cries unto you,' as the Bible says. It is true that the brother spoken of here is Abel and he is quite dead, having been killed by Cain. But the idea is very apt, I think."

"If you were to visit your brother in the south," said Sir Rowan, "I believe Mr. Omsett and I might be able to call on you there. We have talked somewhat of staying at Sissinghurst."

Philippa caught her breath. "Do you mean you would visit us at The Priors?"

"I would hope to have the honour."

"Oh!" exclaimed her ladyship. "In that case, we shall surely go to my brother. I shall not hear of any objections. And you say you will bring Mr. Omsett with you?"

"Mr. Omsett owes me a favour and will be pleased to join me at Sissinghurst," the baronet remarked confidently.

Lady Perrot could hardly contain an impulse to clap her hands with joy. To have her daughters followed into the country by two eligible gentlemen, to have every opportunity of forwarding excellent matches instead of separating the girls from their beaux for a long, tedious summer, to have a good reason to stay out of Scotland, these were blessings not often bestowed upon an anxious mother in this vale of tears.

There was one small difficulty, however: Miss Neville had gone to Kent. Her ladyship had no hope that the young lady would take herself off some place else when she heard who was coming to stay at The Priors. Her presence would make a stay at her brother's house exceedingly awkward.

Well, her ladyship told herself with a sigh, she would simply have to make the best of a bad situation there. She would have to behave in the most friendly manner toward the young woman, as though she had never snubbed her at all, and hope that soon all the ill will between them would be forgotten. Naturally, Miss Neville would be rendered uneasy by Sir Rowan's appearance in Kent. She would not be able to witness the baronet's attentions to Philippa without pain. But that was not Lady Perrot's affair. The young woman would simply have to look out for herself.

CATHERINE DID NOT want for amusement at The Priors. The building and its grounds provided much to explore, to wonder at and to imagine. In the ruins of the old priory, which dated back many centuries, she imagined knights and ladies fair, dragons and castles. She often brought along paper and sketching implements, in case she should feel inspired to draw. Although the ancient arch still standing might be thought to supply an excellent subject for a sketch, she usually ended by writing a poem.

The Jacobean portion of the building and the modern portion, built in the last century, were connected by a Long Gallery. Through this gallery marched tourists from time to time, en route to the Library, the Dining Room, the Drawing Room, and the Saloon, which were open to the public. During her wanderings, Catherine occasionally found herself accosted by a tourist and asked to supply information regarding the collection of books or the dyspeptic-looking faces in the portraits. At such moments, she was required to suppress a strong desire to manufacture a fictional reply. The effort the restraint cost her could be relieved only by the composition of two or three lines of poetry.

The modern portion of the house was a noble edifice of symmetrical grandeur at the summit of a gently falling slope. It had been richly furnished by the third Earl of Ticehurst, who had contrived to purchase each magnificent piece at a bargain. As she wandered among the rooms, Catherine imagined what life had been like under rule of the niggardly third earl, and she imagined the irreverent laughter of her soon-to-be-born niece or nephew echoing through the halls. She hoped the little one would discover the joy of sliding in her stocking feet along the polished floor, as she herself liked to do when no one was about.

Thoughts of Sir Rowan would, of course, obtrude. She did not expect to expel his memory any time soon. But she had every confidence that the deliciousness of solitude, the solace of poetry, the affection of her sister, the kindness of her brother-in-law and the beauty of her surroundings would have her heart patched up and as good as new by summer's end.

Catherine had no sooner drawn this conclusion than her quiet contentment was broken. While she and Anne sat in a sumptuous parlour, engaged in sewing a cushion for a joint-stool, the servant came in bearing the message that Lord Byron had come to call. Anne looked at the card in amazement. "Lord Byron?" she read. "What does he want here?"

Catherine blushed. "I suppose he wishes to call on me. We were acquainted in London."

Motioning to the servant to remove the stool, her ladyship desired his lordship to be shown in. She was curious to see this Lord Byron, of whom she had heard much, none of it very good. She could not help but be astonished that her reserved and retiring sister could know such a man.

Although he walked with a limp, he entered with a graceful, manly stride. When he saw Catherine he stopped, smiled with his dark eyes and bowed. He raised her ladyship's hand to his lips and presented himself, saying, "You will forgive the intrusion, I hope. I was on my way from London to Newstead Abbey and could not pass this way without stopping to ask after Miss Neville."

Anne narrowed her eyes. "Newstead Abbey is in Nottinghamshire, I believe," she said.

"I acknowledge it with pride," he declared.

"That is north, sir. This is south. Either you do not know the way to your own house, or you are lost."

He smiled roguishly at the countess. "There is yet a third possibility, my lady. I may have come all this way with no better excuse than a desire to visit Miss Neville."

Anne was not won over by the man's devilish fine looks. She would not allow herself to be taken in by his charm, his wit or his smile, for she suspected that this was the gentleman who had broken her sister's heart. If he was, she did not wish to be cordial to him.

Catherine had blushed when she first set eyes on her visitor. His appearance suddenly thrust her back in London for an instant. But she contrived to enquire serenely, "Our friends in Town were well when you left them, I trust?"

"Yes. Mogglemere informed me before I left London that they were to dance at Hampstead. I daresay they had a fine time."

"And were they *all* well, Lord and Lady Perrot and their daughters? Mr. Omsett?" Catherine continued. "And Lord Mogglemere?"

"I believe so. Miss Perrot was to dance two dances with Sir Rowan, and her sister Daphne meant to grant a similar favour to Mr. Omsett. Happily, no one is likely to write a review of the result."

At this reference to reviews, Catherine bowed her head, while Byron turned to the countess, wondering if she would take a hint to go off somewhere so that he might have a moment alone with her sister. "I have brought Miss Neville a message from London," he said pointedly, thinking that a sufficient hint. But Lady Ticehurst was either too knowing or too ignorant to recognize it, so that Byron was forced to add, "Will you think me very ill-mannered if I deliver the message to your sister?"

"Not at all," said Anne pleasantly. "I should like to hear it myself."

"The fact is," he countered blithely, "that the message is from me. You see, I have read your sister's sonnets. I was unable to do so before she left Curzon Street, but now that I have, I must speak with her about them."

"Yes, by all means, speak with her."

"I'm afraid you would be bored."

"Not at all. I should be charmed."

He declined to favour her with his famous scowl. Instead he turned to Catherine and said with gentleness, "Miss Neville, I hereby renounce everything I have ever said to you, everything I have ever done in your company. I ought never to have kissed you upon the shoulder. It was very wrong of me, but until I read your poems, I did not know you. Until I read them, I believed you were an ordinary young lady, like every other young lady I have ever known. But now, Miss Neville, having read your poetry, I declare that *this* is the moment of our meeting. This is the moment of our first setting eyes on each other. What an honour it is to meet you, Miss Neville." Here he gazed at her without smiling, then went down on his knees and kissed her hand.

CHAPTER ELEVEN

"THAT IS NOT TO SAY that your verses are free of fault," the poet continued. "One or two suggestions for improvement occurred to me as I read, and I would be pleased to put myself at your disposal, should you care to hear what they are."

As he looked up into her face, Catherine felt a jumble of emotions. One could not help but be flattered by the praise of a young genius, for so Catherine regarded him. One could not help but be flattered by the attentions of a man who was known never to exert himself in regard to women. One could not help but be flattered by his coming so far to see her. But he overwhelmed her, and the excesses of his expression struck her as ridiculous. She would have laughed, had she not caught a charming expression of amusement in his brown eyes. She felt herself drawn to that expression; it reminded her of a light she had often perceived in the eyes of Sir Rowan.

Anne stood and marched to Byron, whom she rapped on the shoulder with her finger and said, "Get up, sir. What if someone should come in and see you looking so foolish?"

Byron rose, and said with a grand flourish and a brilliantly insincere smile, "It appears I was overcome. Perhaps it is the heat of the room. If Miss Neville would kindly show me the grounds, the fresh air would restore me in no time."

"I shall show you the grounds myself," Anne declared. "My sister is hardly familiar with them. Besides, I think she ought to go and get some of her new poems for you to see. You may take them with you when you set forth for Newstead—in an hour."

Grateful for the excuse to escape, Catherine went to fetch her poems, while Anne put her arm on the gentleman's and led him relentlessly through the home park, the woodland walk and the hedge maze. At the end of the hour, Byron surrendered. The countess had won this round, and as a devotee of the art of boxing, he was wise enough to retire to his corner for the nonce, until he should have prepared a strategy to win the next bout. Before he addressed Miss Neville again, he must win over the countess, who had evidently heard of his reputation as a bounder and believed every scrap and tittle of it.

He took his leave of Catherine and her ladyship, and as they watched him mount his horse and gallop away at a dazzling pace, Anne asked, "My dear Cathy, have you decided to tell me what happened in London to send you flying into Kent?"

Catherine sighed. "To speak of it is still painful."

"I see. Well, will you tell me this much—was Lord Byron connected with the affair?"

She nodded. "He was."

With a fierce look in the direction the rider had taken, Anne said, "That is what I thought," and she coaxed her sister into the house as though she were an invalid.

THAT NIGHT she knocked on the door of her husband's dressing room and went inside. As he tied his robe of fine silk, he pleaded with his hounds to vacate the bed. The dogs remained oblivious to his blandishments. "Good evening, my love," he said, looking around and smiling at her.

"You were wrong, Binky," she announced.

At this declaration, his face went white. "I'm terribly sorry, my love. I had no idea. Wrong about what?"

"About Cathy. Her heart has not been broken, at least not yet."

"Well, that is a consolation. An unbroken heart is better than being right, don't you think?"

"Oh, yes, but I believe she is afraid that her heart *will* be broken. I believe she fled London for that very reason. My observation tells me that she is afraid of falling in love with Lord Byron; she knows it will be the ruin of her."

He made kissing sounds at the dogs in his effort to woo them to the floor, but they barely raised their eyelids.

"What is your opinion, my love?" she asked with a sigh. "What ought we to do?"

Called for his opinion twice in the same week, his lordship stood straight and blanched. "My opinion is, my love, that there isn't very much we *can* do."

"Ah, you mean to warn me, do you not? You think that if I interfere, I will drive her straight into Byron's arms? And you are quite right, my love."

"Thank heaven. Here, Tiger. Get down. Good dog. Come on, Viper. Off you go." Although he addressed the animals by their ferocious names, they ignored him placidly.

"Therefore," she said with energy, "we must not appear to be interfering. How can we contrive it, my love?"

If his wife had not been with child, his lordship would certainly have pleaded ignorance. But having heard that women in a delicate condition must be humoured at all costs, he bestirred himself to think. At last he said, "We must interfere in a manner that does not look like interference."

"Yes, I see what you are saying, my love. We must offer Cathy a distraction. There must be enough activity, enough society, to prevent her from thinking of the fellow, or of our stratagems to discourage his addresses."

"Good heavens, what an excellent plan!"

"But where shall we find such activity and society? We are awfully quiet. The village has little to offer, and the local book society would not do, I fear. We need more liveliness than the country hereabouts affords."

"I daresay we shall have to import some liveliness."

The countess beamed as she sat on the bed to pat the dogs. "What an inspiration, my love! We shall invite your sister."

His face took on the expression he usually reserved for twice-boiled chard. "Sally, here?"

"If she and Cathy had quarrelled as I first thought, I would, of course, not propose it. But now I think the expedient will do wonderfully well. Sally will bring her daughters, and their young friends will come calling, and we shall have a house full of merriment and joy. My sister will not have a moment to dwell on thoughts of Byron. With all her friends about her, she will not be tempted in the least."

The earl climbed onto the bed next to the slumbering hounds. "But I don't like my sister," he said.

"Of course not, my love. Neither do I. But that is nothing to the purpose."

"Are you certain we must invite her, my love?"

"I am only following your advice, my love, and very wise advice it is, too." As she rose and walked to the door, her husband tried to think what advice he had given that had led to such a calamitous conclusion. When he could not recall, he gave it up as a bad job.

Turning at the door, the countess bade her husband a sweet night's rest and whispered "Come, come." Instantly, the dogs bounded off the bed and followed her from the room, leaving their master to fret alone.

AT FIRST, the news of the invitation alarmed Catherine. Her last wish was to spend the summer with two women who would not speak to her. Further thought, however, yielded a more rational view of the proposed visit. If the Perrot ladies were still angry with her and did not wish to meet her, they would simply refuse the invitation. If by some chance they accepted, they would not offend the Countess of Ticehurst by cutting her sister, and therefore they would of necessity treat her with cordiality, regardless of the sentiments they cherished in their hearts. Either way, Catherine had no reason to dread a visit. Even the quiet solitude she had enjoyed so blissfully of late would not be disturbed by the onslaught of visitors, for the house was so vast as to permit one to get lost in it for hours and hours.

Although she could look forward to the visit of the Perrots with equanimity, she did not know what to make of Lord Byron's recent call. His flamboyance, his melodrama, his sweeping gestures and naughty smile unsettled her. She could not recall when she had seen him look so handsome or so penetrating. All the time he spoke, she had the feeling that he was taking the measure of her, assessing her, trying to guess whether he wished to fall in love with her.

It had been impossible for her to meet the electric look in his brown eyes, for she felt herself suddenly uncertain. Her late encounter with Sir Rowan had left her shaken. Thank heaven her sister had taken it into her head to do the honours as guide through the grounds. Had she walked alone with the poet, she did not trust herself to know the outcome. And, thank heaven, he had not meant to make any stay in Kent but had left at once for the north. She was not yet ready to deal with flirting gentlemen, and especially not a gentleman whom she admired in many ways, a gentleman who made his admiration of her very evident and who reminded her achingly of the man she was determined to forget.

THE ARRIVAL of the Perrot family was a noisy affair that chased the Earl of Ticehurst from his house. Lord Perrot had not formed one of the party, his wife explained; he preferred to go to Scotland, where he might fish and shoot and smoke cigars and drink his precious port. In his place, her ladyship had brought Lord Mogglemere, who pleased the countess by enquiring particularly after her sister. "Cathy is in the house," she informed her guests. "You will find her in the green saloon. She has tea for all of you."

Entering the saloon, the party came forward one by one to greet Catherine. If there had been any ill will among any of them when she had quit Town, clearly it was now forgotten. Lady Perrot smiled and murmured and squeezed dear Miss Neville's hand as though she were a third daughter.

To Catherine's surprise, Philippa asked her deferentially whether she would favour them on some future occasion with a song on the harp. She knew that Catherine played and so much regretted that she had not had the pleasure of hearing her perform when she lived with them in Curzon Street. "I do not play myself, but know musical taste when I hear it," Miss Perrot simpered. "I cannot abide a performance of any kind unless the execution and tone are admirable, as I've no doubt yours are.''

Lady Perrot applauded the suggestion, saying that she was devoted to the musical arts herself and wished her own daughters could boast the proficiency of an instrument that Miss Neville was reputed to have.

Catherine marvelled at this display of hypocrisy, for neither of them had ever evinced the slightest interest in her musical ability before. However, she considered their sudden professions of interest too amusing not to reward them with generous smiles and a promise to play for them soon.

Seeing that Catherine sat a little apart from the others, Lord Mogglemere moved to sit next to her. ''I expect you have found a good deal of inspiration for your sonnets here in Kent,'' he said. ''Rarely have I seen more beautiful surroundings.''

''Why, yes, I have no want of subject here.''

''Oh, I am sure you will not soon exhaust the beauties of the place. We saw a pretty Greek temple in the distance along the approach to the house, as well as a fine deer park and a duck pond teeming with swans.''

At the mention of swans, Catherine excused herself to fill her teacup. Before she could return to her seat, the countess addressed her guests thusly: ''My dear friends, now we are gathered together, I wish us all to be as jolly as we can be. Therefore, let us lose no further time in entertaining ourselves.''

This invitation to mirth cast an instant pall over the company. The ladies and his lordship looked from one to another, wondering what specifically the countess had in view. None of them had any objection to amusement, but they were hard-pressed to know how to go about getting some. Gloom crossed their faces as they contemplated the necessity of being jolly.

Daphne suggested that they might play a game of riddles, a suggestion that was greeted with silence.

Philippa offered to read from Cicero, but Daphne moaned an objection.

Lord Mogglemere thought they were all very jolly just as they were. He did not see why the generality of people thought it necessary to be always going and doing. Some people could not abide stillness and silence, he said as he rose and began to pace in front of the window drape. "As to stillness and silence, there is nothing I treasure more. It is the height of folly to rattle on with nothing to say simply to fill a void of silence, which might be perfectly charming, if one remained still and silent long enough to enjoy it."

This speech left them still and silent for a considerable time, until Lady Perrot observed that if Miss Neville would play for them now, it would undoubtedly be a spark to conversation, for whenever she was in a room in which someone sat down to play, the talk instantly grew louder and more convivial.

Catherine excused herself on the pretext of having letters to write, and Anne was left to wonder how to transform such a dull company into the sort of distraction that would keep her sister from being seduced by a bounder.

A WEEK LATER, the same company, with the addition of the earl, sat in the green saloon on a rainy, dreary day, still discussing ways in which they might be jolly. Lord Mogglemere and the Perrot ladies played at cards. Catherine sat at a small corner table, making a fair copy of some lines she had recently composed. The master of the house dozed, as did his hounds, and his lady shifted about in her chair, sitting being an uncomfortable activity in her condition, especially when performed in the company of such dullards.

Into this quiet scene came the footman with the announcement that two gentlemen had come to call on Lady Perrot. Impatiently, Anne urged them to be brought in at once. Any diversion was welcome, but the diversion of two gentlemen who had travelled in all this weather to call on them was as curious as it was welcome.

The gentlemen did not disappoint her curiosity. The first to enter, Mr. Anthony Omsett, was a fine-looking, amiable young man with an air of modesty as well as breeding. And she was struck at once by the gentleman who followed Mr. Omsett into the room. No sooner had Sir Rowan Heath been presented to her than she decided that he was the very man to save her sister from Lord Byron, for his air, his manner, his figure, and his countenance were all superior to anything she had seen in some time.

Sir Rowan's entrance brought the room suddenly to life. Both Binky and the dogs awoke. The former shook his old chum's hand with pleasure, and the latter saw at once that he knew the precise spot on the neck where they liked to be rubbed. Philippa blushed with pleasure to see him, and Lady Perrot beamed, for the compliment of the call must be all to herself and her daughters. As Daphne leapt up to greet Mr. Omsett and to take possession of him, the countess invited Sir Rowan to sit by her and partake of some refreshment.

The instant she heard his name, Catherine blotted the page she was writing and nearly overset the ink pot. It infuriated her that even after all this time, she could not be tranquil in his presence. Scolding herself, she made a determined effort at composure, then set her fair copy to rights again. She took the time to nod a greeting to each of the gentlemen as they were presented to her, then returned to her labours with fierce concentration.

Whereas five minutes earlier, the atmosphere in the room had been generally dispirited, it was now animated. The cards were put aside. Everyone gathered to talk with Sir Rowan and, more especially, to have the pleasure of hearing him talk; everyone, that is, except Daphne and Tony Omsett, who took themselves off to a window seat to enjoy the view of the rain, and Catherine, who sat in her corner, writing steadily, without once pausing to mend her pen.

The first impression Sir Rowan had of the room when he entered was that Catherine was uneasy. This presented him with a dilemma. If he was to prove to her that her ease of mind was of foremost concern to him, ought he not to leave at once and spare her the distress of his company? On the other hand, if he did quit the house, how would he begin to carry out his plan? It gave him pain to see her uneasy. He would have given much to be able to go to her, take her hand and talk to her soothingly. But it appeared they were both going to have to endure a good deal of uneasiness, for he was not about to turn back now.

In the course of the conversation, the countess gleaned from her sister-in-law some particulars regarding Sir Rowan. She learned that he was a baronet of good blood and fortune and with no reputation for gambling or running up debt. He was engaged in the heroic enterprise of writing political essays, an endeavour which frequently brought him into danger of his life, though, naturally, he laughed at the very mention of danger. And, her ladyship added, he was soon to be engaged to her eldest daughter. This last confidence the countess chose to dismiss. She had quite another destiny in mind for Sir Rowan Heath. Smiling at the gentleman, Anne caught his eye and enquired into his lodgings in the neighbourhood.

"We have put up at Sissinghurst, which is highly satisfactory," said Sir Rowan.

"Oh, but it is too far," Anne objected. "The roads will be muddy and full of potholes after this rain. You will have a dreadful time of it, travelling in a coach."

"You are very good to concern yourself with our welfare," said the baronet. He glanced at Catherine, who, he knew, must overhear every word that passed their lips. What was she thinking? he wondered.

"I am also concerned with my own welfare," declared the countess. "If the distance is too great, and the roads are too bad, then you will not wish to visit us, and then I should be desolate."

Sir Rowan assured her that if the roads did not permit them to travel comfortably by carriage, they would come on horseback.

Lady Perrot and Philippa exulted in this declaration. It signalled the baronet's determination to be wherever they were.

"I could not ask you to ride out in such weather," Anne said. "You will both catch your death. Binky, my love, what is your opinion of Sir Rowan's lodging so far from us?"

The earl looked up from the animal whose belly he petted and opened his mouth, hoping an answer would issue from it. At last he surprised himself by saying, "I think they lodge too far from us, my love."

"I think you have hit on it exactly, my love."

"Have I? Well, there you are, then!"

"Yes, I think the gentlemen ought to come to us. Goodness knows, we have enough room. Two guests more will not inconvenience us in the least. In fact, the addition of two gentlemen will be just what is wanted to make us jolly."

Sir Rowan paused. He had resigned himself to making Catherine uneasy with regard to his visits to The Priors. But what would it be like for her, knowing that he slept under the same roof, might turn a corner at any moment, might be placed next to her at dinner? He could not accept the countess's invitation until he had considered how his presence would affect Catherine. At the same time, he did not know how to refuse such an opportunity to be near her.

"You are most kind, my lady," he told his hostess. "I will take a moment, if I may, to consult Mr. Omsett on the matter."

Here he rose and approached Tony and Daphne, who were engrossed in gazing into each other's eyes.

"A word with you, old fellow," said Sir Rowan, interrupting.

Daphne had the good grace to appear to blush and tottered off to leave the gentlemen to themselves. When he had explained his dilemma to Tony, Sir Rowan asked, "Do I dare accept?"

"I hope you will. My flirtation with Miss Daphne Perrot proceeds apace, and if I were here on the spot, I daresay I should probably persuade her to kiss me."

"Tony, my good man, you are not supposed to be forwarding your own lovemaking here. Your purpose is to forward mine. If you recall, it is owing to your good offices that I am in this fix to begin with. Now, what are we to do?"

"I don't know, Heath. It's a wonder you ask me after what I did. I vow, I am the last man I should trust were I in your shoes."

Sir Rowan nodded. "You are right. There is only one person who will tell me truthfully what is the right thing to do." Here he turned and moved with determination toward Catherine.

Sensing a shadow by her elbow, Catherine looked up to see Sir Rowan gazing down at her.

"May I sit a moment?" he asked.

She nodded, put a blotting paper on her page and closed her book.

The baronet deduced from this action that she meant to hide what she had written from his satiric eye. It was a slight action, but one that gave him a pang. Nevertheless, he brought a chair near to hers and sat down. "I imagine you heard what transpired just now. Your sister very kindly invited Mr. Omsett and myself to stay at The Priors."

"Yes, I did hear."

"I cannot accept, nor can Mr. Omsett, until I know your feeling on the matter. If our coming to stay would discompose you, then we shall not come."

Although she could not look at him, Catherine was grateful for his consideration. She had not thought him capable of it, and was glad to be proved wrong. Unfortunately, she did not know whether she could reward his consideration by saying that he might accept the invitation. She could not deny that his staying would discompose her. That is, she could deny it, but she could not mean it.

"Cathy!" her sister called to her, causing her to start. "Cathy, you must tell Sir Rowan to come to us."

She looked at him, feeling trapped.

Anne called again from her chair, and this time she waved her arms by way of punctuation. "Sister, you must persuade him to come, and Mr. Omsett, too, for if they will consent to join us, I know exactly how we may be jolly."

"There is an inn not far from here—The Blue Bottle, I believe it is called," Catherine answered.

"That will never do!" cried the countess. "It is a perfect hole of an inn. I have not seen the place, but I am sure it is rife with bedbugs. No, they must stay here. For what I propose, they must stay here."

"Then I suppose you must accept the invitation," Catherine said to Sir Rowan, endeavouring to resign herself to difficult days ahead.

"Well, do you not want to know what it is I propose?" Anne asked her sister. Then, addressing the company at large, she asked the question again, "Are you not curious to know what it is I mean to do with all of you?"

CHAPTER TWELVE

RELIEVED THAT HIS LADY had asked a question that did not call for him to deliver an opinion, the earl answered that he was very curious indeed to know what she had in view.

"Amateur theatricals," came the answer.

This announcement was greeted by a murmur. The idea of performing intimidated most of the company.

"I don't know anything about acting a part," said Philippa. "I fear I should blush every time I was supposed to make a speech."

Lord Mogglemere shook his head doubtfully. "I have heard that to act a play, one must commit a great many words to memory. How is it possible to remember them all?"

"I should not like to dress in an unfashionable costume," Daphne declared. "I should be mortified to appear as a witch or as someone who wears blue."

"You needn't fret, any of you," the countess assured them. "I shall take care to see that you are all delighted with everything. You will not be asked to play any role that will put you to the blush, and I shall supply magnificent costumes, in colours most fashionable and flattering. I shall select a play and say who will perform the roles so that my excellent company of players will not be inconvenienced by the want of a stage manager. As to the conning of the words, I beg you not to be alarmed at the prospect, Lord Mogglemere. I shall allow you to carry your speeches with you on the stage, if need be. Your reading from a paper will not detract in the least from the jollity, I promise, for this is to be a private theatrical, and we may do exactly as we please."

As none of the others put forward any further objection, Anne was at liberty to pursue her plan, and pursue it she did. Her object was to find a way of throwing Sir Rowan and Catherine together as much as possible in an atmosphere conducive to falling madly in love. She could think of no better atmosphere than that of a romantical comedy. A play, after all, required rehearsal. The actors must be constantly in one another's company, speaking lines of the most intimate nature. The portrayal of tender lovers could not fail to awaken like feelings in the players.

ON THE FOLLOWING DAY, when all the company were gathered in the sumptuous, candlelit dining room, the countess announced that the play was to be *Twelfth Night*.

"Ah, Shakespeare," Philippa said glowingly. Then abruptly she frowned. "But surely you do not mean us to enact a comedy. While I admire the nobility of Shakespeare's language, as everyone must, it is frequently improper in the comedies."

"I shall take out the improper parts," Anne said. Here she signalled the footman to serve out the potatoes and boiled vegetables.

Sir Rowan asked, "I wonder where we shall find actors to fill all the roles. We have the three ladies we require, but are lacking several gentlemen, I believe."

The countess shrugged and laughed. "I shall take those parts out, too."

"What a pity," the baronet answered. "Well, I hope you will not excise Malvolio, for he is as fine a villain as ever I saw." Then, turning to his left, he addressed Catherine. "I should make an excellent villain. Do you not think so, Miss Neville?" He studied her face in anticipation of the answer.

"I have always felt very sorry for Malvolio," Catherine said with her eyes fixed on a slice of roast fowl. "When he is confined to prison and so cruelly abused, I cannot help but pity him. Shakespeare cannot have meant us to laugh at Malvolio in those scenes of torture."

"I am glad to hear," Sir Rowan said softly, "that you can find it in your heart to pity a villain," and there was something in his warm tone as he said it that caused Catherine to colour.

"I do not know whether I shall keep the villain in the play or not," Anne declared. "If gentlemen are scarce, which they always seem to be in these warring times, then we shall have to dispense with some of the roles. I should be just as happy to do without a villain. What is your opinion, my love?"

After a pause, the earl declared, "My opinion is that a villain is a disagreeable fellow."

"There, that disposes of Malvolio," said the countess. She whispered directions to the footman in regard to the sauces, puddings and jellies, then attended to the conversation again.

"Could not the ladies play gentlemen's roles?" Daphne asked. "In that way, we might have enough players, and no one would be without a part."

"An excellent expedient," Sir Rowan said. "In Shakespeare's day, boys took the young ladies' roles; in our time, why should we not employ the reverse method?"

Anne giggled. "It is done! I shall play Sir Toby Belch. I would not ask any of my guests to play the part of such a reveller; therefore, I must do it myself."

Lady Perrot put in here, "I do not wish to mar your joy, but I must excuse myself from assuming any role. I become tongue-tied if I am required to make a speech I have learnt by heart."

"Good Lord, Sally, you have never been tongue-tied in your life!" cried her brother with more truth than politeness.

"If you prefer not to speak a part," said Anne soothingly, "then you shall not speak a part. I shall dress you in a pretty yellow gown and you shall hold a lace fan. We shall make you a lady's attendant, and you shall not be obliged to say a word unless you wish to."

"How kind of you, my dear. If you like," Lady Perrot said, "I shall send for Perrot. He will leave his fishing, or whatever it is he does in Scotland, as soon as I tell him he is wanted here. He will even take part if I tell him to."

But the countess did not think such an extreme measure necessary.

"What do you think of this scheme of the countess's?" Sir Rowan asked Catherine in a low voice.

"I think it makes my sister happy and whiles away the time until her confinement."

"You have answered for your sister, not for yourself."

"I like a play well enough" was all that she said, for the subject put her in mind of the last time she had seen a play and the conversation that had taken place in the chandeliered hall at Covent Garden.

"There, now everything is splendid!" Anne said. Contentedly she watched the dishes served out in abundance and the smiles of her companions. The company was instructed to meet the next morning in the old drawing room. That part of the Jacobean wing was unused and would serve as a theatre for them in the next weeks. They must all be prepared tomorrow to hear what roles they would play, and they must all be prepared to be vastly surprised.

As INSTRUCTED, the players appeared in the old drawing room to hear the countess pronounce their fate. Her appointment of the *Dramatis Personae* was as follows:

VIOLA, shipwrecked on
the isle of Illyria .... Miss Catherine Neville

ORSINO, Duke of Illyria .... Sir Rowan Heath

SEBASTIAN, twin brother
to Viola .... Lord Mogglemere

ANTONIO, friend
to Sebastian .... Mr. Anthony Omsett

SEA CAPTAIN, friend
to Viola .... Mr. Anthony Omsett

OLIVIA, a noble lady .... Miss Philippa Perrot

MARIA, Olivia's wench .... Miss Daphne Perrot

ATTENDANT, Olivia's
attendant .... Lady Perrot

SIR TOBY BELCH,
Olivia's uncle .... The Countess of Ticehurst

SIR ANDREW AGUECHEEK,
a quarrelsome knight .... The Earl of Ticehurst

"You have eliminated the clown?" asked Sir Rowan. "Will you cancel his songs and wit as you have our villain's villainy?"

At these questions, Anne grew worried. "If you think the clown very important, I suppose I can ask Lady Perrot to send for his lordship."

The baronet shook his head. "Perhaps it would be better to do without Feste the Clown altogether than to have him abysmally miscast."

"I do not wish to disappoint you if you wish to retain the clown," Anne said. "I have promised to keep you all happy, and I mean to keep my promise. Perhaps we may send to the village for someone to sing the clown's songs. I believe the greengrocer is thought to have a fine voice. He certainly sings loudly enough in church. Meanwhile, let us attend to those we have on hand."

Mr. Anthony Omsett was then congratulated on his dual role as friend to each of the twins. As Antonio, he would be black-bearded, rough faced, and softhearted. Then, as the Sea Captain, he would be white bearded, rough faced, and softhearted. The versatility such roles demanded was remarked upon by all, which gave Tony the opportunity to note how well applause agreed with him.

Philippa pouted when she saw that she was to play opposite Lord Mogglemere. She had had high hopes of playing Viola and of speaking Shakespeare's most exquisite sentiments to Sir Rowan. On second thought, however, she was grateful to be Olivia, for she knew she did not appear to advantage dressed in boy's clothing. Viola had to don her male disguise in the first act and was obliged to walk, talk and act like a man until the curtain fell at the end of the play. Philippa would have been mortified if Sir Rowan were to see her wearing stockings and a doublet. Her frame was square and awkward, the sort of imposing figure that required the refinement of beautiful gowns to set it off to advantage. With such thoughts she was reconciled to playing her part and consoled herself with the reflection that whatever her role, she would be allowed to quote Shakespeare with impunity.

In his turn, Lord Mogglemere was also disappointed at first in his role, not only because he was not cast as the Duke, opposite Miss Neville, but also because he was cast as Miss Neville's twin brother. The two could not look more different, as Daphne Perrot pointed out with great glee.

"Why, Lord Mogglemere is tall as a post, thin as a stick, and redheaded as a carrot," Daphne laughed. "Miss Neville, in contrast, is of medium stature and quite fair. As to thinness, I daresay, even in a tailored coat, no one would ever mistake Miss Neville for a boy!"

Sir Rowan saw that Catherine bore the teasing with good spirits and therefore he permitted himself to smile. He had not the least objection to the casting, and he trusted that he and Miss Neville would repair often to the theatre for the purpose of rehearsing their lines.

The earl ventured a whisper to Anne when he learned what part he was to play. "This fellow Aguecheek has an odd propensity to challenge everyone he meets to a duel, my love."

"Yes, you read his character aright, my love. You are a clever thing, you are."

"I think the gentleman's a fool, my love, for all he is a knight. Why should one quarrel when it is just as simple to agree with one's companions?"

"Not everyone is as congenial as you are, my love," his wife whispered back. "But this is a play. You are only pretending to be quarrelsome."

"But why can I not pretend to be a pleasant, agreeable fellow?"

"If I can pretend to be an uncouth drunkard, surely you can pretend to be quarrelsome, my love!"

"Yes, my love, but in the scene which you showed me, I am required to quarrel with Cathy. I should never dream of quarrelling with your sister, as you well know. You would have my hide if I did."

"I shall have your hide if you do not, my love, for the play is so written."

He shrugged and gave himself up for lost.

Daphne had a complaint, as well: that she was asked to play the part of a servant. "I am sure if Philippa is to play a noble lady, I ought to play one, too."

"But there is only one noble lady in the play," Anne said.

"I am sure I can play a noble lady as well as Philippa," she responded with a tearful sniff.

"Have you read Maria's lines?" Sir Rowan asked Daphne. "If you have, then you know that she is a beautiful, mischievous, intelligent and admirable young woman. She is certainly one of the liveliest females ever to grace the stage."

"Is she?" Daphne asked in wonder. "Then I suppose I am content with her, so long as she does not wear blue."

Turning to Catherine, Sir Rowan said, "Are you pleased with Viola?"

Catherine answered with an appearance of calm. "As pleased as I can be. I do not know how long it is since you have read the play, but you may recall that Viola disguises herself as a young gentleman, and the Duke sends the young gentleman to woo Olivia for him. What this amounts to is that I am about to spend the better part of the summer making love to Miss Philippa Perrot!''

He laughed. Their eyes met, and she could not help laughing with him. Then suddenly conscious of his eyes on her, she grew serious. As lightly as she could, she said, "I daresay it is just a lark and as soon as we have had all the amusement we can get out of it, we shall abandon the project."

"I suspect you are right," said the baronet. "Still, I wish the villain had not been banished from the play. Without him, we shall be forced to take out half the comical scenes."

"Perhaps you would play a dual role, in the manner of Mr. Omsett. If memory serves me, the Duke and Malvolio never appear on stage together. Therefore, you may play both the hero and the villain at once."

She looked up at him, expecting him to laugh again, but his expression was so serious that she was startled. It occurred to her that what she had just said had wounded him, and she felt too confused to say more.

He was the first to recover, remarking, "I shall make the suggestion to your sister." On that, he moved toward the countess and was instantly replaced at Catherine's side by Lord Mogglemere.

"Alas, this is a monstrous imposition on you, I fear," he said to her. "When will you have a moment to write a sonnet?"

She regarded the tall, redheaded gentleman with a smile. In London, she had scarcely been able to tolerate his solicitude. Now, having fallen in love, fled from her lover, and met her lover again face-to-face, she had a new appreciation of his concern. She felt a kind, peaceful emotion, which she prized after the tumultuous emotions she had so recently experienced. She was grateful to his lordship for his solicitude, and thus she said to him with gentle patience, "Now that you are my brother—my twin brother—we must not concern ourselves with rhymes and jingles. Our sole purpose is to reunite our family and see that everybody lives happily ever after."

With this new view of the matter, Lord Mogglemere was induced to recover from his fit of the sullens and to regard himself as uncommonly fortunate in having the opportunity of being so nearly related to the fair Miss Neville.

ANNE CONSENTED to have Sir Rowan enact both the hero and the villain. She also sent to the village for the greengrocer, who, it developed, was too overcome by the honour of associating with the quality to have any voice left to him. When it turned out he could produce no more than a terrified squeak for the countess, Catherine took pity on him and begged that he be allowed to return home. They would have summoned the baker or the haberdasher to play the clown, but Sir Rowan tactfully reminded them that a private theatrical would no longer be private if villagers were brought in and that the result might be gossip. Thanking the baronet, Anne declared that they would dispense with the clown. The loss would not matter greatly, she declared, as they had gained a villain in his place.

At the first rehearsal, Anne distributed bits and pieces of costume. Her husband, as Sir Andrew Aguecheek, was dressed in a pink feathered hat and given a monstrously heavy sword to carry. Tony Omsett wore a thick black belt as one sea captain and a thick white one as the other. Maria, the servant girl, wore ribbons and sashes of lavender, Daphne's favourite colour, while the Lady

Olivia—Miss Philippa Perrot—wrapped herself in a regal shawl threaded with gold and silver. As the Duke, Sir Rowan wore a cloak of lush green velvet; as the villain, his cloak was coarse, plain and black. For the part of Viola, the young woman disguised as a young man, Catherine wore blue breeches and stockings and a flowing blouse of white. Anne's own costume consisted of a large-brimmed hat such as Sir Walter Raleigh might have affected.

Having dressed the members of her cast, the countess sent them to various rooms in the household, all except the Duke and Viola, whom she put through their paces in the drawing room. She passed over the first three scenes in Act One, promising to return to them at another time. It was necessary, she said, to begin with the most difficult scene.

"It is hardly difficult," Catherine pointed out. "It is only a few lines."

"You are right," her sister said. "We must therefore rehearse two scenes at once. Now, you will be so kind as to speak your lines."

Here she seated herself in a sturdy Hepplewhite chair and gestured to Catherine and Sir Rowan to stand by the window curtain where a goodly space had been cleared for a stage.

Lord Mogglemere poked his head in the door and was told to go away. The earl also appeared with a question and was barked at for his trouble. At last, there was quiet enough to let the rehearsal go forth, which it did, with a peremptory, expressionless reading.

"Dear me," Anne complained, "I am sure you cannot be reading the same *Twelfth Night* I have before me. My Duke Orsino speaks with a depth of passion. The Duke is a feeling man."

Sir Rowan laughed. "He is too feeling by half, your ladyship. He is positively lovesick."

Anne sat bolt upright. "That is unkind, I am sure."

Here they looked at Catherine for her opinion on the matter. "Dearest Anne, I'm afraid Sir Rowan is right," she said. "The Duke is lovesick. But you are also right, for he is noble and good. He must be, for Viola is a sensible young woman and would not love him otherwise."

"If I play Orsino with an excess of feeling," Sir Rowan said to the countess, "his lovesickness will be the more repulsive. Let me subdue it a little with a subdued performance."

"But Sir Rowan," Anne said reasonably, "if you were in love with a young lady and she refused you, would you not be overwhelmed with grief? Would you not lie about and listen to sweet music and sigh a good deal? I am sure that is what a rejected lover ought to do."

"I would do nothing of the kind, my lady," he said. Here he walked to Anne.

Catherine could not help drawing closer to hear what he would say.

"If I were in love with a young lady and she refused me, I would not lie on my pallet and moan like a puppy. I would do what I could to be near her. Unlike the Duke, I would never send another man to speak for me. Only an ass would do such a thing! He deserves to lose Olivia if he cannot go to her himself."

Here Catherine could not help asking, "But if you went to the young lady yourself, what would you say?"

He turned to her to answer, "I would say nothing."

"Oh," said Catherine, though she could not explain why she felt such disappointment at this answer.

Anne watched the two as they conversed, and it appeared to her that they spoke with a good deal more intensity than she had dared to hope for at this point. Evidently, her stratagem of producing a play was succeeding already.

Sir Rowan went on, "I would say nothing because words are meaningless. I would *show* her that I love her and mean to make her happy all her days."

"How would you contrive to show her such a thing?"

"I would seek her out whenever possible so that she might see by my conduct, by my manner, what my feelings are. If she fled the town, I would follow her to the country, and I would persist, regardless of how long I was required to be patient."

With considerable emotion, she said, "You surprise me, Sir Rowan. Surely a man of the world such as yourself would not wish to waste his time wooing a lady who continually spurned his addresses. I should like to believe your professions, but I find it impossible."

Now Anne was hearing in their words much of the passion she had wished for earlier. She sat down again to watch her sister and the baronet.

He came to Catherine. "But you must believe them," he said urgently. "A woman of understanding must see beneath appearances. She must know that a man may appear in charity with all the world and still suffer."

Breathing too hard to speak, Catherine closed her eyes and looked away. His message was unmistakable, and it made her reproach herself. She had failed to see what he was suffering. The charge hurt and angered her, though she could not tell whom she was angry at—Sir Rowan or herself. In another moment, if she did not act soon, he would see her tears. To prevent that, she straightened her shoulders and went quickly from the room.

Seeing her leave, Sir Rowan took himself severely to task. He had provoked Catherine, even though he had made a solemn vow to be all that was gentle and soothing. Angrily, he flung his velvet cloak to the floor and stalked off, as well.

All in all, Anne concluded, the rehearsal had gone off beautifully, for when a man and a woman disagreed as hotly as Sir Rowan and Catherine had, they were well on the road to falling in love.

CHAPTER THIRTEEN

AT THE NEXT day's rehearsal, Duke Orsino coldly informed a very stiff Viola that no woman could possibly love with the passion that beat in his male breast. Women "'lack retention,'" he stated sharply. "'Alas, their love may be called appetite.'" In contrast, he said, the love he felt was "'as hungry as the sea.'" Then he turned his back on her.

Sir Rowan's tone as he levelled these sneers pleased Anne mightily. Although the play called for the Duke to sound melancholy, the countess much preferred Sir Rowan's indignation. It was an excellent sign of his being in a state of high emotion.

Viola's reply also pleased the lady. It was spoken bitterly and asserted that women were every jot "'as true of heart'" as men. Her tone ought to have been sweet; however, the countess relished its vigorous antipathy. Nothing was so much a spur to love as hatred. When Viola crossed to the Duke's side so that she faced him squarely, the countess had the pleasure of seeing the two glare at each other with fiery looks.

The actors continued in this vein for some time. The countess concluded that it would not be long before their feelings became too excruciating to be contained. Consequently, she considered it best to remove herself quietly from the theatre in advance of the explosion, confident that if she left them to themselves, her sister would surely end up in the baronet's arms. As quietly as she could, she tiptoed out the door and made for the parlour at the end of the gallery.

Unaware that they had been left alone, Sir Rowan and Catherine embarked with a not very good grace upon the final scene of the play. Viola untied her pale gold hair and let it tumble to her shoulders, thus revealing her true identity as a woman. She performed this action not as though she meant to enlighten the man she loved, but as though she meant to punish him. As she waited for him to reply, she breathed deeply.

At the sight of the heroine's loosened hair and glowing eyes, the Duke paused. It was only with an effort that he managed to read the line asking if it was possible she had loved him all this time.

Her eyes flashing, her voice full of venom, Viola replied that she had indeed loved him all this time.

At this avowal, the Duke put his hand to his temple. Then, with a glance at his copy of the playbook, which he held in one hand, he reached out the other, saying, "'Give me thy hand, and let me see thee in thy woman's weeds.'" He took a moment to observe her closely in her woman's weeds, then another moment. With difficulty, he returned to his text, but what he saw there prevented him from going further.

Catherine, too, stopped. The stage direction in her copy had been crossed out. Instead of taking her hand, as the dialogue prescribed, new words directed Orsino to kiss her.

Sir Rowan glanced at Catherine's playbook, then again at his own. The identical words appeared in both copies. The new direction had been penned in a fair hand.

Astonished, they turned to where Anne had stood just minutes before and found she had gone. It took them less than an instant to guess that the countess had written in the new direction and then absconded before the event. It was too transparent a trick, and too entertaining a one, for Sir Rowan to continue frowning. He began to laugh his deep, manly laugh.

Catherine held herself rigid until laughter got the better of her, too. She looked at Sir Rowan with more appreciative mischief in her eyes than he had seen since their time together in London. Her loosened hair he could withstand. Her boy's costume, her soft voice, her electric presence—all these he could withstand. But he could not hold out against her eyes alight with mischief.

He drew her into his arms and kissed her achingly. Helpless, she felt the pull of him, so that it took all her strength to keep from forgetting what divided them. She did not trust herself to maintain her composure and knew that if she did not escape at once, her resolve would fail her utterly.

As soon as he felt her resist, he released her. She said nothing in answer to the intentness of his eyes, only dropped her playbook and moved toward the door. She would have left him without a word, but Sir Rowan caught her by the hand.

"Just hear me out," he said, "and I will let you go." It was more of a command than a plea. "This will not happen again, I promise you. I shall go at once and insist on being given another role. Lord Mogglemere will be eager to exchange with me, I've no doubt. It shall be done immediately."

He did not stay to receive a response but walked out the door to seek the countess. When he had gone, Catherine impatiently brushed tears from her cheeks and upbraided herself for behaving like a foolish female.

THE PARLOUR at the end of the gallery served as a theatre for Lord Mogglemere and Philippa. They had repaired to that room the moment the countess had made it clear that the old drawing room, like her attention, was reserved for Viola and the Duke. They had assisted each other in learning their cues, then in memorizing their lines. Lord Mogglemere was amazed at the vast number of lines Miss Perrot was required to learn, and when he saw how quickly she contrived to commit them to memory, he began to see the young woman in a new light. "I had no idea," he told her, "that you were possessed of such gifts."

Flattered by this commendation, Philippa assisted his lordship in conning Sebastian's part. First she located a pen, then neatly inscribed scratches beneath every word he was supposed to utter. When he saw that his lines stood out from all the others, he felt greatly relieved and was able to read his speeches without confusing them with anyone else's. To Miss Perrot he felt he owed this small but happy triumph.

As they sat on the sofa that morning, reading one of the scenes, their elbows happened to touch. They sprang apart with such a start that they could not resume their rehearsal on the same easy basis they had become accustomed to. On the contrary, they could scarcely concentrate on their lines for wondering if their elbows would touch again.

Taking a breath to still her pounding heart, Philippa suggested that Lord Mogglemere inject a bit more expression in pronouncing the well-known line, "If it be thus to dream, still let me sleep!"

He repeated the line several times after her, each time imitating her variety of pitch and tone. As he did so, he found himself watching her lips, while she watched his. Soon their lips were moving in unison.

Then his lordship clapped a hand over his mouth.

"What is it?" Philippa cried.

"I never knew it before," he said hoarsely.

"Knew what, my lord?"

"Why you were always so fond of quoting. But now I do. I mean, once one has gone to all the trouble of learning the words, well, one may as well put them to good use!"

So moved was Philippa at this sudden understanding between them that she let fall a tear. Seeing it, his lordship apologized for offending her.

"No, no. It is only that I am accustomed to being ridiculed for my extensive use of quotation. My mother and sister have forbidden me to employ any extract in the company of gentlemen."

Gently he said, "Perhaps they have never had to sit two days and learn a speech by heart before. No doubt if they did, they would not wish to waste it." He took her hand and patted it.

Blushing, she looked down at his long fingers knocking against her knuckles.

Seeing her blush, he blushed. All at once, he took her by the shoulders and exclaimed, "My dear Miss Perrot, if you know any famous sentiment regarding a kiss, I beg you will recite it at once, for after you say it, I mean to do it."

Before Philippa could think of an appropriate extract, the countess burst in. "Good morning," she said. "I am glad to see you busy rehearsing. It would not do for the Duke and Viola to be the only ones rehearsing. Now, how far have we come?"

She spent a considerable time hearing their speeches, unaware that they wished her on the other side of the world, or at least the other side of the house. Trying not to look at each other or to fidget or to sigh, the young man and woman obeyed the countess's directions mechanically, and for their efforts won her high praise.

At last, Anne made as if to leave them, and they anticipated taking up their discussion where they had left off, but Sir Rowan interrupted. "Madam," he addressed the countess gravely from the doorway, "I am unable to play Duke Orsino and beg you will allow me to exchange roles with his lordship here."

Horrified, Anne objected, "But you've almost learnt the lines, sir."

"True, but I shall learn the new ones as well."

"I cannot allow you to change."

"You must. I have discovered that the villain and the Duke appear on stage together in the final scene of the play. As I cannot be in two places at the same time, I must give up one of the roles. I will gladly give up Orsino, knowing how much Mogglemere would like to play him."

"We shall eliminate the villain's lines at the end of the play," Anne countered. "Villains add nothing to happy endings, in my estimation, and may be dispensed with."

Mogglemere rose to add his protest. "See here, I like Sebastian very well now. Miss Perrot has been so kind as to translate everything the fellow has to say. I cannot go learning a new role now when the old one has just been made intelligible."

The baronet paused a moment to think. At last he said, "Very well, if Mogglemere does not wish to give up Sebastian, perhaps Miss Perrot would be good enough to give up Olivia. I make no doubt that Miss Neville will be delighted to exchange roles."

His listeners deduced from his remark that he had quarrelled with his leading lady and wished to be rid of her.

Anne put her hands to her cheeks, distraught at the failure of her plan. She could not understand how things could have gone awry. She had left Sir Rowan and Cathy in the most promising state, speaking their lines at each other as though hurling slings and arrows. Instead of behaving as they ought and falling in love, they were giving up their roles, which was the last thing the countess wanted.

A new thought occurred to Anne. Perhaps if she did not appease Sir Rowan in this, he would pack his valises and remove to Sissinghurst. One had only to look at the set of his square jaw to know that either he or Catherine would have to have a new part. Gritting her teeth, therefore, she affixed a smile to her lips and asked Philippa, "Would you be so gracious as to step into Viola's role? I fear that our little scheme of a private theatrical will go to pieces if you do not."

Philippa was torn. She did not wish to give up Olivia now that she and Lord Mogglemere were on such excellent terms. Nor did she wish him to see her in boy's attire any more than she had wished Sir Rowan to see her. At the same time, she did not wish the play to be abandoned. It offered too much delicious opportunity for her to spend time in the company of his lordship. Moreover, Viola had very fine lines to speak, not so many as Olivia perhaps, but many more worth quoting.

"I should be so particularly grateful if you would consent," said the countess. "We must find a way out of Sir Rowan's difficulty."

Looking at Lord Mogglemere, Miss Perrot said deferentially, "What do you think I ought to do?"

He screwed his face into a thoughtful expression. "I think that if you do choose to be Viola, you ought to permit me to rehearse you in your cues and your speeches, for I do not know how you will get on if you do not have assistance."

This offer pleased Philippa so greatly that she gazed into his lordship's eyes for a considerable time. He gazed back, so that it was not lost on either Anne or Sir Rowan that the two had suddenly conceived a tendre for each other.

Anne felt irritated at the sight of the lovers. She had gone to much trouble to throw Catherine and the baronet together, to manoeuvre them into roles that must spark their sensibilities, and to leave them alone. The upshot was they they were further apart than they had been before she had interfered. Meanwhile, Miss Perrot and his lordship, without any assistance from her, had fallen head over ears in love. It was maddening.

Sir Rowan observed the lovers in a different light. He began to regret that he had asked Miss Perrot to assume Viola's role. For her to do so must of necessity separate her a good deal of the time from Mogglemere. The notion of separating two people who loved each other was particularly repugnant to him just now, and therefore, he said gently to Miss Perrot, "It was improper of me to make such a request. I withdraw it. I shall find another means of dealing with the difficulty. Mr. Omsett and I shall exchange roles."

"But I do not mind, really," Philippa assured him. "As long as Lord Mogglemere will engage to assist me, I should like to play Viola. However, I have one stipulation."

"What is it now?" Anne cried in vexation. "It seems no matter what lengths I go to to please everybody, no one is satisfied."

"It is only this, my lady. I wish to appear in a very long tunic, as long as my gown."

The countess rolled her eyes to heaven. "You may appear in peacock feathers and nose rings if you like."

Philippa sighed contentedly, smiling at his lordship, thinking that she was the most fortunate creature on the face of the earth. "A long tunic will do very nicely, I thank you," she said and opened her playbook to Viola's first scene.

CATHERINE STOOD in the centre of the enormous old drawing room. Apart from the curtains, an odd assortment of chairs, and bits of costuming thrown over a table, it was empty of furnishings. It was a perfect theatre, dusty, grey and lonely. Although the summer's warmth filled the air, the room struck her as chilly, and she shivered. What Sir Rowan had said upon leaving had worked powerfully on her. His consideration, his concern had all been for her. He had taken upon himself the task of finding an actor to play opposite her, not for his own sake, it was clear, but for hers, so that she would "not have to endure this sort of thing again."

As she recollected the warmth of his declaration, his words of the day before came back to her. He had upbraided her for not seeing beneath appearances, for taking his insouciance as a mirror of his feelings, for failing to acknowledge that it was possible for a man to suffer as well as a woman. And he had been right. She had done him an injustice. In everything he had said to her since coming to The Priors, even in his angriest moment, he had shown himself to be profoundly interested in her well-being, and he had done so in a feeling, not a care-less manner.

Sick at heart, she sat down heavily on one of the chairs to think. How would she be able to thank him for his consideration? They were not on speaking terms. How would she right the wrong she had done him? He would no longer be nearby at every moment for the purpose of rehearsing. How would she speak gently to him and tell him she was sorry for what she had said? He had had too much evidence of her dislike to give her so much as an opening.

Her eyes fell on her playbook, which lay open on the floor. The last page of the last scene stared up at her. A closer look told her that the scrawled words "They kiss" had been written in a familiar hand. She recognized her sister's squat, curlicued style, and she took a breath.

So her sister had been plotting against her. How ironic. Well, she supposed it was to be expected. Had she been open with Anne to begin with, had she told her of the re-lations that had existed between Sir Rowan and herself in London, no misunderstanding would have followed. She had no one to thank for her present straits but herself.

Again her eyes fell on the page. Again she observed the words that had been inked in, and her imagination leapt to the image those words provoked. It brought back to her sensations she had thought dead, and she was too honest not to acknowledge that they were very much alive.

THE PARTY that gathered in the green saloon after din-ner was subdued. Tony Omsett and Daphne took them-selves off to the window seat and ignored the others. If the sole topic of their earnest whispers was *Twelfth Night*, their companions would have been very much surprised.

Lord Mogglemere and Philippa sat on a sofa with a copy of the play between them. Each took turns holding the book and showing it to the other. Frequently they forgot what they were speaking of, allowed their elbows accidentally to touch and then giggled.

The Countess of Ticehurst regarded these loving pairs with disgust. She had looked forward to having visitors, to the distraction good company would offer her sister, and to the liveliness it would supply her while she grew too large to get about as she liked. Now, it turned out, visitors did nothing but plague one. They took it into their heads to follow their own silly notions instead of looking out for their own best interest. It was futile to try and do a favour for anyone, even one's own sister. One only ended up disappointed. She ought to have listened to her husband.

"You were right, my love," she told the earl in a low voice.

He awoke from his doze. "Good Lord! I was? Well, I am glad to have been of service, my love."

"You were not of service, because I did not listen to you."

"Oh. What was it I said?"

"You said I ought not to interfere with Cathy, that I ought to leave her in peace."

His lordship could not recall ever having said anything of the kind. Nevertheless, rather than distress his wife with the truth, he took the credit for such a wise injunction. "Perhaps it is not too late, my love," he suggested. "Perhaps we may still leave her in peace."

She sighed heavily and shook her head. "It is too late, my love. It is all up with us, and I can do no more. My punishment is that I am condemned to watch these infernal lovers, pining and mooning round every corner of my house.''

Here he took her hand in his and rubbed it soothingly. "If you want my opinion, my love, you take too gloomy a view. I do not know what the matter is, but if you want my opinion, it cannot be as bad as you think.''

"I do not want your opinion, my love.''

Hearing that for once his opinion was not wanted, the earl was greatly pleased. Contentedly, he remained silent the rest of the evening, bestirring himself only to rub his wife's hand and pat his dogs' bellies.

Lady Perrot saw with amazement that her elder daughter had been smitten with the charms of Lord Mogglemere. She had not had any inkling of their ever noticing each other before. At first, she regarded their mutual sighs and glances in disbelief, recalling that in London Lord Mogglemere's indifference to Philippa had been equal only to her indifference to him.

But it was the work of a moment to become reconciled to the exchange of Sir Rowan for his lordship. An earl always got the preference over a baronet in Lady Perrot's book, even though the latter might be richer. And Sir Rowan habitually wrote those Whiggish political essays that smacked thoroughly, in her husband's estimation, of change, progress and suchlike nonsense. Lord Mogglemere, thank heaven, was sensible enough not to concern himself with politics. Moreover, Sir Rowan had not shown any peculiar regard for Philippa since his arrival in Kent, whereas his lordship had obviously been wounded by Cupid's sharpest dart. He now demonstrated as much solicitude for Miss Perrot's gift of extraction as he once had shown for Miss Neville's muse. Thus did Lady Perrot teach herself to think that Lord

Mogglemere would answer her matrimonial hopes for her daughter as well as any baronet.

Sir Rowan purposely sat in a chair as far from Catherine's as possible. He glanced from time to time at a newspaper, thinking restlessly of the news of the day, of the number of weeks until Parliament resumed, and of the lively debates at Child's. Frequently, though, his thoughts dwelt on the softness of Catherine's profile. As she concentrated on her embroidery, her bare neck bent gracefully and her cheeks glowed. It was not possible to observe her thus occupied and not attempt to talk with her. Consequently, he rose and walked to her chair, asking if he might be permitted to sit. She gazed up at him with shining eyes, but he did not appear to notice, so engrossed was he in what he was about to say.

"I was unable to persuade Lord Mogglemere to take on the role of the Duke," he informed her. "Therefore, I did the next best thing. Miss Perrot has consented to be Viola. I hope that will answer our difficulty."

The smile she had allowed full expression now faded. "Miss Perrot?"

"Yes. It was most kind of her, I think, and I have thanked her. I know you will also be grateful to the young lady. She has relieved you of the burden of rehearsing day and night with Orsino."

Catherine felt heat colour her face. Sharply, she said, "You will now rehearse with Miss Perrot day and night, I collect."

He looked at her, puzzled. Once, long ago, she had spoken of Miss Perrot in that tone of pique and he had recognized its source as jealousy. For a moment, he allowed himself to hope; then he quickly dispelled the hope. She could no more be jealous of Philippa than she could still be in love with him. Therefore, he said, "Miss

Perrot and I will rehearse as often as necessary, I suppose."

"It will not do," she said to him in a whisper that he found remarkable in its intensity. "Miss Perrot is in love with you."

He smiled and shook his head. "Miss Perrot's heart is safe from me, I assure you."

Urgently, she said, "You have been so kind, so thoughtful where I am concerned. I beg you to think now of Miss Perrot. Do not permit her to take this role in the play. The result will be disastrous. She will nurture her affection for you, and when she discovers that you do not return it, it will be too late for her to recover. Believe me when I tell you that one does not soon or easily recover from such an affection."

He did not know how to reply. It seemed to him obvious that the lovebirds on the sofa were so lost in each other's longing gazes as to remove all doubt as to the object of Miss Perrot's affection. Catherine, who was every bit as observant as he was, ought to have seen it. She hadn't, however, and he thought it odd. If she had missed what was so blatantly clear, it could only be because she was too absorbed in her own feelings. What were those feelings? To what extent was he concerned in them? If those feelings were anxious and distressful, would it be best for him to leave The Priors?

Gravely, he said to her, "Perhaps I ought to leave your sister's house. I have already caused enough difficulty and do not wish to cause any more. It appears I ought to go."

For an instant, Catherine's old shyness overtook her and she could not find the voice to urge him to stay. Then, a desperate courage rescued her, and she would have seized his arm and asked him not to go, but there was suddenly a noisy stir in the room, which caused them both to look up.

A visitor was announced, and then, with the flash and electricity he never failed to generate, Lord Byron entered the room.

CHAPTER FOURTEEN

THE COUNTESS nearly wept. This was all that was wanting, she thought miserably—for her sister's would-be seducer to walk through the door. She received Byron's flourish of a bow with a disdainful nod and watched as he approached each of the ladies in turn to kiss their hands. He spoke one or two private words to Catherine, after which Sir Rowan stood up from his chair and left the room. Catherine appeared tense, as though the arrival of the newcomer had quite overset her.

His greetings completed, Byron approached the countess and paid her his compliments.

"So you have come all the way from the north to visit us," she said irritably.

"Yes, and with your worthy husband's permission, I shall sit just here, so that we may talk."

As the worthy Earl of Ticehurst was engaged in snoring and whistling in tune to his dogs, he made no objection to Byron's sitting.

Anne favoured Byron with a scowl. This was invitation enough. Lifting his coattails in back, he lowered himself into a chair opposite her. Impudently, he grinned. "I have an odd suspicion you do not like me," he said.

"It would be dishonest in me not to confirm that suspicion," she replied.

"I thank you for your candour. One meets with so little of it in the world that one must admire it, even when it is practiced to one's own detriment."

"Do not dare toad-eat me, young man. I know very well you are making up to me."

He laughed. "I knew you would prove a shrewd antagonist, and that is why I wish to make a friend of you, if I may."

"I do not wish to be your friend. I have heard that you have the knack of ruining your friends."

"Madam, you are too wise to heed vicious gossip. No, there is another reason for your unaccountable dislike of me."

She raised her eyebrows. "Unaccountable, you say? It is not the least unaccountable. You are a brash puppy. You are arrogant, dissolute and false."

"Yes, I am all those things, but I am also persistent, and I shall sit here and force you to be hospitable to me until you tell me the truth."

There was enough charm in this speech, and in the naughty look he wore, to prompt Anne to respond, "Very well. I dislike you on my sister's account. It is because of you that she fled London."

His initial response was surprise. Then he smiled. "Far be it from me to contradict a beautiful lady, but you are mistaken. Your sister may have fled London, but not because of me."

Anne looked at him in bewilderment. "But did you not make love to her and cause her to fear for her heart?"

"I should have liked nothing better, but she had other matters to bedevil her. Did she not tell you?"

"Tell me what?"

"That Sir Rowan Heath wrote a scathing review of her book of poems, a review that was somewhat talked of in Town and caused her considerable mortification."

The countess looked at her sister, who had put aside her embroidery and was staring ahead at nothing in particular.

"Good God. She was running from Sir Rowan!" cried Anne. "And I threw her together with him at every opportunity, the man she most hated in all the world!"

"You threw them together? How on earth did you contrive to do that?"

"We were to have amateur theatricals. Heaven help me, I cast my sister as the heroine and Sir Rowan as the hero."

He laughed again. "How charming. I am certain they were vastly amused."

"They nearly cut each other's throats."

"Did that not give you a hint of their feelings?"

"I thought it meant that they liked each other."

Maintaining a serious expression, he said, "Such an error is entirely understandable. I've known many lovers who looked as if they wished to cut each other's throat."

"But what is to be done? I have made a dreadful muddle of the business."

"I hope you will allow me to help you out of this muddle, my lady. I believe I know what is to be done."

Anne regarded him with a more charitable expression than she had been used to directing at him. It bespoke remorse instead of suspicion. "I don't know why you should come to my aid. I have not been very cordial where you are concerned."

"Perhaps that is why. I am too used to being lionized wherever I go. The last time I paid you a call, you were so original as to toss me out on my ear."

"By saying so, you encourage me to go on abusing you, and just when I had begun to like you very well."

"There is no one whose abuse would delight me more; however, we have more serious matters at hand. You must replace Sir Rowan in the play at once. You must allow me to play opposite your sister. And if I may be permitted to say so, I shall not make you ashamed to have appointed me the hero."

"A replacement has already been accomplished, in a manner of speaking. Sir Rowan insisted I give his role to Mogglemere, and when I did not, he saw to it that there was a new Viola—Miss Philippa Perrot."

Byron grimaced. A picture formed in his mind. He saw himself playing Orsino opposite the prosy young woman who sat by Mogglemere. "As Miss Neville has been replaced," he said, "you must allow me to do what I can in the way of distracting her from thoughts of Sir Rowan. I should like to invite her to think of poetry instead."

"Yes, she ought not to be frittering her time away at theatricals. She ought to be writing sonnets."

"Exactly. And my fortuitous appearance will be justification for her doing so. As you may recall, you sent me packing with some of her poems. I have read them, and I have much to say to her about them."

With a grateful sigh, Anne said, "Indeed it *was* a fortuitous appearance. I don't know what might have happened if you had not come when you did. For all we know, Cathy might have hit Sir Rowan. She was that angry with him, you know, though I really did think she admired him. No man is so admirable to a woman as the one best able to drive her to distraction."

"There is much wisdom in what you say, madam. Mayhap your sister will learn to be so driven by someone who is truly worthy of her, and not a mere writer of reviews."

"Yes, well, if you could contrive to distract her, then I trust her heart will soon heal and she may meet with some gentleman such as you describe."

Satisfied to have garnered the countess's trust, his lordship congratulated himself on winning the round. He now looked to win the match. Thus, he remarked to her, "It is unfortunate that I am required to put up at your village public house. The Blue Bottle, I believe it is called. It is not as handy to The Priors as one would wish; nor can it be called commodious, even by such a fantastical fellow as myself."

Anne nodded. "It is a veritable hole. No human creature ought to have to sleep in such a vile place. No, you must remove at once to us."

"At once? But the hour is late, my lady."

"Lord Byron, do you think I am still in leading strings? Do you expect me to believe that you ever get to bed before dawn?"

"Ah, my lady, you see right through me. I can never hope to pull the wool over your eyes, can I? Very well, I shall come to you and the earl there this very night." Immediately he sought out a servant. Instructions were given to have his things brought at once to The Priors. That done, he stood at the door post and watched Catherine. A few minutes was all he required to assure himself that her charms had not suffered as a result of her recent travails as heroine in a play. Therefore, he went to sit by her side.

Catherine's thoughts were riveted on Sir Rowan. Where was he now? When did he mean to leave The Priors? Would she ever see him again? When she looked round, she was astonished to find that Lord Byron was speaking to her and that his subject was her poetry. She looked at him without seeing him, listened without hearing him. As he rose, he brought her hand to his lips and murmured, "Until tomorrow, then." She saw him go to her sister, whisper something that prompted Anne to smile, and then resume his seat next to her as though he were quite at home.

CATHERINE LAY AWAKE in her bed, watching the candle burn low. It seemed to her that her former shyness had overtaken her at exactly the wrong time, that she ought somehow to have responded to Sir Rowan's announcement, that she ought to have said straight out that she wished he would not go. The disruption caused by Lord Byron's entrance had prevented her from speaking. Still, if she had been able to summon the courage, the courage that had sustained her many times in London, she might have acted.

How she might have acted she hardly knew. She could not very well have followed the baronet out of the saloon. It would have looked very particular. It would have mortified Anne, and caused the others in the room to drop their jaws. And yet, would that shame have pained her worse than the shame she now felt? She was ashamed of having sat still and silent, ashamed of having doubted him, ashamed at having extended to him none of the courtesy he had extended to her.

But if she was ashamed of her own conduct, she was proud of his. He had deliberately put himself in the way of meeting her again, though he risked her continued rejection. It was not the sort of thing a man of Sir Rowan's reputed carelessness ordinarily went to the trouble of doing. Moreover, he had demonstrated at every turn that his first thought was for her ease of mind. All of it said to her that he loved her still.

Once again she found herself wishing that she had followed him out of the room. Surely, impropriety in that instance would have constituted no great crime against Kingdom or Crown. There were those who would have remarked upon it, of course, but what did she care for their gossip? And if to follow him were no great crime, to send a note to him by the servant could not be any worse. She would merely have to dash a few words to him on a paper, just enough to persuade him to stay. Of course, she had never before been so bold as to send a note to a gentleman by way of a servant, but she understood it was done all the time. One of the chief uses of servants in plays, it seemed, was to run back and forth between the hero and heroine delivering notes.

She climbed down from her bed to take up her writing desk and scrawl a note. But the pen point broke and she could not find the right words, and by the time she had mended the implement, she felt that whatever she wrote must be either too much or too little. She replaced the pen and paper in the desk and sighed. What good was it to be a poet if one had nothing to say for oneself at such a moment?

At last, she found a shawl, wrapped it round her and went to the door. Straightening her shoulders, she opened it and peeked outside. The corridor was empty. Taking her candle, she tiptoed over the carpeting, wishing that the candle were not so brilliantly reflected in the mirrors and chandeliers, hoping that no one would suddenly issue from one of the doors, requiring her to invent a reason to be creeping about the house in her nightclothes just hours before dawn.

When she rapped on the door, she found that it fell open of its own accord. She stepped inside and held the candle up. In the circle of light it cast, she saw the empty bed. Sir Rowan had apparently not slept in it. Walking to the wardrobe, she opened one of the doors and found it empty, too. The tables were bare of items belonging to a gentleman. Not a shred of clothing, not a scrap of anything belonging to him had been left behind.

SIR ROWAN RAPPED softly with his walking stick on Tony Omset's door. At last, the yawning young editor of *The Gentleman's Review* appeared holding aloft a sputtering candle. "What are you doing here?" he asked, looking at Sir Rowan's travelling dress and riding boots.

"I am surprised to find you here, old fellow. I thought you would surely have taken Miss Daphne Perrot for a look at the stars. Is not Venus in the ascendant tonight?"

Tony beckoned the baronet to come inside. "Do not joke about Miss Daphne Perrot, Heath. I am thinking of asking her to marry me."

Sir Rowan regarded him with a cynical eye.

"I know what that look means," Tony responded, pouting. "You think I am young and unsteady and that she is young and silly."

"I think you will suit each other wonderfully well."

"Do you really, Heath? You are not just quizzing me?"

The baronet fixed his friend with a smile that was uncharacteristically soft. "I wish you very happy, Tony. Indeed, I do." He clapped him warmly on the shoulder.

"Now, goodbye, old fellow. I must go." He went to the door.

Mr. Omsett followed. "Go where?"

"My valet is seeing to my valises. The coach is waiting."

"You are leaving The Priors? At this hour?"

"I do not like skulking off in the dead of night. Still, it seems best not to linger."

"Where will you go?"

"I will stop overnight at an inn, and tomorrow go on to Cheshire. I have neglected my farms and house long enough."

Tony could scarcely read Sir Rowan's expression in the dim candlefire. "But why? I thought you were amused by the play. I thought you meant to win back Miss Neville. I thought she was pleased to see you again."

"Wrong on all counts, dear boy. My presence here does nothing but give Miss Neville pain. So I am removing myself forthwith."

"I must say, I think you are mistaken."

"You are mistaken in thinking I am mistaken."

"But if she were so displeased with you, why did she consent to play Viola? She might have persuaded her sister to choose a different actress, or a different Orsino, or a different play. But she let it all go forward. I cannot believe she would have done so if she had not wished for your presence."

Sir Rowan gave this observation close thought, then said, "I should like to believe you are right, but I can't. You see, I told her I meant to leave and she said nothing to prevent me."

"I have noticed that Miss Neville is occasionally shy. I daresay she would not be the first poet to be more at ease with pen and paper than with speech."

The baronet regarded his friend seriously, then smiled. "I vow, you are a clear-headed fellow for so early in the morning. What have you to drink here? I have a mind to hear more along these lines."

Tony located a decanter which contained two drops of brandy, poured himself and his guest a meagre glass, then, as Sir Rowan availed himself of a chair, he reclined on the bed to see what his imagination might next inspire him to say of an encouraging nature.

HURRYING BACK to her chamber, Catherine was astonished, and not a little annoyed, to find Lord Byron poking about her door. He was no less astonished to find her on the outside of it instead of the inside. "It is no wonder you did not answer my knock," he said, with an appreciative glance at her nightdress.

"What are you doing here?"

"I might ask you the same question."

"I asked you first."

"If I tell, will you tell?" He grinned with a charmingly wicked grin.

"Oh, very well."

Here his lordship was forced to call upon his vast reservoir of invention to answer, "I was sure I heard noises, strange noises. I came out to investigate. Yes, that's it, I wished to see if the ghost of an old prior or prioress haunted these gilded halls."

"I suppose you must have heard me moving about. When I could not sleep, I attempted to write a few lines, but found I could not."

"Ah, so you thought to go for a little stroll instead. It is all perfectly clear to me now."

"I do not stroll about the corridors at dawn, my lord! I leave that sort of thing to gothic heroines."

"A wise stratagem. But what were you doing, that is to say, what *are* you doing out here?"

She blushed, but said forthrightly, "I had heard that Sir Rowan had left the house, and I went to see if it was true."

"And what did you find?"

"It is true."

"Well, no doubt he has not gone far."

"Why do you say that? Do you know where he has gone? If you do, I beg you will tell me, for I must speak with him."

Lord Byron cleared his throat. He regarded the young woman, huddled with her shawl around her soft nightdress, looking chilled and irresistible. Not a trace of neck or ankle did her clothing reveal; yet she was more alluring to him than many a female he'd been privileged to view in deshabille. With a sigh, he endeavoured to seek out his better nature, so as to preserve this fresh flower from despoilation. "I really ought to say nothing at all," he told her with an effort.

Her hand clasped his lapel. "You must tell me, Lord Byron. If you know where he is and do not say so, I shall never forgive you."

Such earnestness succeeded in overpowering what little there was of the gentleman's better nature. Helplessly, he said, "I believe I heard him say that he meant to go to the Blue Bottle."

With a nod, she thanked him and made as if to enter her chamber.

"Wait," he said. "Do you mean to go to the Blue Bottle?"

"Naturally."

"I cannot permit you to journey there alone. Heaven knows what manner of indignity you would be subjected to in such a place. I shall go with you."

She sank against the door, her eyes full and shining. "Do you mean you would put yourself to so much inconvenience? How good you are," she murmured.

If she had not turned then to go inside, his better nature might have vanished entirely.

TONY OMSETT HAD JUST located a full decanter of brandy in the library when he heard a stirring outside the door. Opening it, he stepped into the hall to find Miss Neville in pelisse and bonnet, making for the entrance.

"Good morning, Miss Neville," he said uncertainly. "That is, good night. That is, I do not know what to wish you. It is too late, that is too early, to still be night, yet I cannot think it morning until it is actually light."

"How do you do, Mr. Omsett?" she replied. Aware that it must look very odd for her to appear dressed for going out at such an hour, she thought it best to make as little of it as possible.

"I felt a bit restless tonight," he said, holding up the decanter for her to see. "Apparently you did, too. You have decided to go for an early outing, I collect."

"Yes."

"Are poets often subject to fits of this sort?"

"I suppose they are. May I ask, Mr. Omsett, if Sir Rowan told you that he meant to quit The Priors?"

"Why, yes."

"Did he happen to to say where he meant to go?"

"He said he would stop at an inn, then travel to Cheshire."

"I see."

"Miss Neville, are you certain you wish to venture out tonight? Poetry or not, the air is dreadfully damp, and your sister will be worried when she hears of your excursion."

"You may tell my sister I have dressed against the dampness."

"But she will not know where you have gone."

"I expect I shall return before she knows I have gone, but in case I do not, you may tell her I have gone to the Blue Bottle."

"Indeed! But she will worry that you have gone to such a place alone."

"You may put her mind at ease by telling her I have not gone alone, that I have gone with Lord Byron."

Tony had drunk only the tiniest bit of brandy and knew his head was not befuddled. He must have heard correctly. Miss Neville expected to put her sister's mind at rest by leaving word that she had gone out to an inn with England's foremost scoundrel! He put his hand to his temple. Why on earth would Miss Neville do such a thing, and at such an hour?

Here the servant came in to say that his lordship awaited her at the carriage. Taking a hurried leave, Catherine went on her way, while Tony uncorked the decanter and took a long drink. He could not believe his ill luck. He had just spent the better part of an hour endeavouring to convince Sir Rowan that Miss Neville loved him. Now, he had just discovered, she was in love—or fancied herself in love—with Byron. Many women of his acquaintance had assured him that Byron was devilishly handsome and irresistibly charming when he exerted himself to be, but he could never see what they saw to like in him. Miss Neville was the last young woman he would have expected to be taken in by such a fellow.

How could he go back to his chamber and tell Sir Rowan what he had just seen? The baronet would very likely get that murderous gleam in his eye and heaven knew what might follow from that. But if he did not tell the baronet and the baronet found out, then he would direct that murderous gleam on him, young and hopeful Anthony Omsett, a literary light, soon to be engaged, a promising gentleman with everything to live for.

CHAPTER FIFTEEN

WHEN THEY ARRIVED at the Blue Bottle, Catherine could hardly wait for Byron to hand her out of the carriage. She hurried into the public room, boldly looking about her. Although the hall was lit, there was not a face to be seen save that of the publican, who rested it on a table in contented sleep.

"Miss Neville," Byron whispered, "you must not stay here. I shall bespeak us a parlour."

Immediately he poked the innkeeper and informed him that he would have the best private room the place afforded. After the man had finished rubbing his eyes, Byron folded a coin into his hand. At this, the landlord's eyes opened at once and he led the gentleman and lady to an oaken room with a small table, three chairs and a fireplace with a cold, empty grate.

"Rest yourself, Miss Neville," Byron entreated. "Remove your pelisse and hat. Let me help you take them off. Do sit down. I shall send for something to drink."

She neither sat nor removed her pelisse. "I must enquire after Sir Rowan," she said anxiously. "That is why I am here."

"You must permit me to make the enquiries. It would not do for the Countess of Ticehurst's sister to be seen asking after a gentleman at this hour of the morning."

"Then go quickly. He may have already set out for Cheshire."

Byron took off his cloak, tossed it on a chair and went from the room, rubbing his cold hands. In the hall, he leaned against a post, hummed a snatch of song, then strolled into the public room, where once again he woke the innkeeper. When he had told the fellow what refreshments he required, he returned to the hall in leisurely fashion and sang to himself "Robin Adair" before opening the door to the parlour.

Upon entering, he reported, "The landlord says he believes a gentleman of Sir Rowan's appearance and bearing did bespeak a room last night. However, the gentleman gave orders that he was not to be wakened on any account. The landlord will not tell me what room he is in. I expect he thinks I will attempt to wake him."

"What shall we do?" Catherine cried.

Byron appraised her tensely clutched fingers, which remained gloved, and her still buttoned pelisse. "I think it best that we stay here until Sir Rowan rises," he said. "The landlord promises to inform me the instant he comes down."

"He will not forget, will he?"

"No. I have given him a handsome bribe and expect he will keep his word."

"Well, then," said Catherine, sitting down, "what shall we do with ourselves until then?"

Byron was not a praying man, but at this question he raised his eyes to heaven in thanks. "We shall have the innkeeper light us a fire," he said. "Then we shall get that pelisse and hat off and permit you to be more at your ease."

Catherine looked up to find the gentleman regarding her very much the way a fox regards a chicken. Suddenly conscious of the impropriety of her situation, she replied, "I am perfectly at my ease."

Here the publican entered with some wine and glasses on a tray. Setting them down, he threw two logs onto the grate and lit a fire. He then turned to observe the lady and gentleman who occupied the parlour, looking them up and down as though he knew they were up to no good, and sauntered out.

The landlord's smirk again brought home to Catherine the fact that her coming to the Blue Bottle with Lord Byron was imprudent in the extreme, and that following Sir Rowan out of the green saloon or tapping on his chamber door in the middle of the night was nothing to what she was doing at this moment. She hoped with all her heart that Sir Rowan would awaken with the first light of day.

Sighing, she looked up to find the poet kneeling at her feet and gently nibbling her fingers.

"You are making love to me, sir!" she said.

"I confess it." He leaned toward her to nibble her ear.

His behaviour put her forcibly in mind of the rudeness she had oft been subjected to in Town. Her old shyness, which had lately returned to plague her, now dissipated. Firmly, she said, "You must be very bored if you can think of no better way of passing the time than this."

"I am not the least bored," he purred. "Nor do I intend that you shall be." Standing, he attempted to draw her up, too, but she remained determined to stay where she was.

For a time, they struggled. Byron held her arms, attempting to pull her to her feet. She resisted. After some time spent in this manner, she saw that desperate measures were called for. Consequently, she looked up into his brown eyes, half closed her own blue ones, and said huskily, "My lord, I wish to ask you a question."

"Anything," he said, still pulling her.

Still resisting, she said, "May I rely on your honour, sir?"

Something in her beguiling tone induced him to pull even more urgently. He grunted as he declared ardently, "Whatever honour I possess, it is yours, madam, to rely upon or do anything else you like with it."

She sought out his eyes with an earnest appeal. "Tell me, my lord, on your honour, what did you really think of my poems?"

Instantly he gave up the struggle, dropping her hands and stepping back. His expression became serious. The poet in him now overcame the man. No matter how deceitful the latter, the former could not be anything but true. "Your poems!" he repeated, raking his hands through his hair and pacing. "Your poems."

"Are they worthy, in your estimation, to be called poems?"

He paused to think before speaking. "I must confess, to my ear they had a peculiar music—a melancholy music. But it was not enough. I wanted more from them. I wanted more from *you*."

She was not surprised to hear that he wanted more from her. She ought to have known as much before she set forth with him to the Blue Bottle. Slowly, she estimated the distance from her chair to the door.

"You do contrive to avoid an excess of sentiment, which I admire," he said, "but your verses have one fault."

He paced so close to her that she dared not make a run for it. She knew she must bide her time. He had already become deeply engrossed in his review of her sonnets. In fact, he hardly looked at her at all, so rapt was he in his critique. With any luck, the subject would keep him distracted until the landlord announced that Sir Rowan had awakened.

"Your fault is this," Byron said. "You are too mild." Here he whipped around and gestured wildly with his arms. "Your music hints that it could be wild, that *you* could be wild. You ought to be wild, you know."

She swallowed, afraid that he might be seized with an inspiration to take his own advice.

He came toward her, his face tense with concentration. "You are too polite. You must allow yourself to be vulgar. You are too elevating. You must allow yourself to be harsh. You are too clever. You must allow yourself to be passionate."

He seized her hands so that she could not help but stand. She saw that he was overcome with the force of his own words and therefore ventured to ask, "Does that mean you do not like my poems?"

He threw his hands in the air. "Like? It is not a question of *like*! It is a question of *life*! You are too tasteful. You must be gloomy, as life is gloomy. You are too cheerful. You must be brutal, as life is brutal."

"I see. Well, if you will ask the landlord to bring us pen and paper, I shall sit down and write you something perfectly gloomy and brutal."

He rushed to the door to do as she bade him, then suddenly turned round and looked broodingly at her. All at once he entreated, "A kiss before I leave thee."

"But do you really think kissing is conducive to gloom and brutality?" she asked. "It seems to me it rather dispels the mood we are trying to achieve."

He came toward her. "Bother the mood. If you must be tasteful and cheerful, so be it. I have endured worse."

Here he took her by the waist, pulled her to him and would certainly have kissed her had not the door burst open with a terrific noise and a coarse voice shouted, "Yer a dead man!"

They looked toward the doorway. Filling it was a bearded old yeoman wearing a motley array of rags and carrying a cudgel. His dirty face, ill-assorted dress and swinging cudgel caused Catherine and Byron to stare. The fellow lumbered into the room, fixing Byron with a menacing eye. Suddenly he grasped the poet's arm so that he winced. "Make yer peace," the yeoman growled. "Confess yer sins afore I do ye."

"Confess my sins? My good fellow, we shall be here a month," Byron retorted, wincing in the man's grip.

"I mean to separate yer ears from yer 'ed."

"May I at least be told why I am to be submitted to such a dissection?"

"Ye've run off with my daughter, that's why."

"Why on earth should I run off with your daughter? I have enough to vex me as it is."

"Tell me what ye've done with 'er, or I'll murder ye afore ye can blink an eye."

"Look at this lady, you fool. Is this your daughter?"

The yeoman regarded Catherine through squinting, heavily browed eyes. Roughly, he let go of Byron, sending him flying to the other side of the parlour. Catherine stepped forward to permit the man a clearer look at her.

"That ain't 'er," announced the yeoman. Seeing that he had mistaken the lady, he bowed his head in sorrow. All at once, he threw the cudgel on the table. He touched his hand to his hat in a sign of respect, bowed his head low and made his apologies. "If ye ain't got me daughter," he said darkly, "then she's lost, she is. Me child is lost." Despairingly, he availed himself of a chair and sat down, sinking his head into his hands.

"If she's lost, hadn't you better go and find her?" Byron urged.

"What's the good of it?" the father mourned. "She's gone off with a rogue like yerself, meanin' no offence, sir."

"No offence taken," Byron said irritably. "But you can't stay here. You must go after her. There is no time to lose."

The yeoman shook his head woefully. "It's too late. When the swan sings, it's already dead an' done fer."

"Swan?" Catherine repeated, inspecting the yeoman closely.

Seeing her approach nearer, he pulled his hat down on his head and pulled himself up from the chair. "I'll go, then," he said, "but first, I'm obliged to say a word to the lady, if yer worship pleases."

Catherine waited with curiosity for him to address her.

"I am to go now, miss," he said. "I urge ye, if ye've run away from yer father or yer family, think better of it now. Go 'ome and don't break yer poor father's 'eart."

She tried to think what she might say to reassure the man, but she stopped. The yeoman's costume, it occurred to her, looked strangely familiar. Indeed, as she looked a second time, she recollected a black cloak worn by Malvolio, a white belt worn by the Sea Captain and a broad-brimmed hat worn by Sir Toby Belch. She turned her face away to suppress a smile.

"Very well, old man," she said, "I shall go home, but on condition that you will take me there."

The yeoman hesitated, then bowed his assent.

"Would you be so good as to wait outside for me?" Catherine requested.

He glanced from her to Byron. Then, silently, he withdrew.

Byron regarded her in disbelief. "Miss Neville, do you seriously mean to leave? Do you not wish to discuss your poems? I thought you were here to discuss your poems."

"I have not forgotten why I came here, my lord. It appears I have accomplished my purpose, and so I bid you good night, or good morning, rather." She went to the door.

Byron followed. "But you cannot go off with a stranger!" he exclaimed. "It is neither sensible nor safe."

She smiled at him. "If I had any sense or if I feared for my safety, would I have come here tonight with you?" On that, she opened the door and went out.

THE YEOMAN HAD WAITED for her and now led her out to his cart. After helping her aboard, he asked her to name their destination. He appeared very much awed to hear that he was to drive her to the best house in the county. The sun was rising in the sky as they set forth on the road to The Priors.

He said nothing as they drove, so that it was left to Catherine to attempt conversation. "You must permit me to express my sorrow at the tragedy of your daughter's flight," she said.

He grunted.

"It touches my heart to see your despair. In truth, the sight of it makes me regret that I ever was so foolish as to go to an inn with the gentleman who accompanied me."

"I should think you would regret it!" the yeoman said angrily.

Catherine smiled at the sound of that anger. "You must love your daughter very much to come after her as you did."

He shrugged.

"I'm sure if she knew how much you love her, she would return to you at once."

He shouted something unintelligible to the horses.

"When I saw you, I was reminded most vividly of my own father," she went on. "He is long since dead, but while he lived, he was a dear and good man, a man I might confide in, a man a daughter might say anything to and be understood."

"Pity he ain't alive. E'd give ye a good 'orsewhippin' fer runnin' off with that blagguard."

"And when I saw you, I thought to myself, why *there* is a man to whom I could speak as I would speak to my own father. I could tell you, for instance, that the reason I came to the inn was to find a man—a man named Sir Rowan Heath."

This news induced the yeoman to glance at her quickly, then grip the reins and urge the horses forward.

"You see, Sir Rowan and I were engaged once, but I broke the engagement. I won't belabour the reasons. But I have since come to see that he is the very man to make me happy. And I believe that I could make him happy, too, if he would let me."

She waited for a reply but, to her disappointment, none came. "How can I tell him of my change of heart?" she asked.

He remained silent.

"Please, what do you advise me to do?"

"If yer askin' me advice, then it's this," he said harshly. "Ferget the gentleman an' find another. Not that scalliwag at the Bottle, but another, a worthy man to make ye 'appy."

This was not at all the reply Catherine had looked for. It distressed her that Sir Rowan would acknowledge neither his identity nor the avowal she had just made. She began to wonder if, instead of being too shy, she was not shy enough, if she had behaved too boldly, if all she had accomplished by this night's work was to give him the opportunity to spurn her as she had spurned him.

They spoke no more during the remainder of the journey, and when they parted at the house, they did not say so much as goodbye.

HALF AN HOUR LATER, the following note was brought to Catherine in her bedchamber:

My dear Miss Neville,
Before I was to leave The Priors, word came to me that you had left the protection of your sister's house to accompany Lord Byron to the Blue Bottle. Knowing what he is and that your association with him must necessarily affect your reputation, regardless of whether or not you were able to maintain your virtue, I resolved to follow you to the inn.

My purpose was to persuade you to return to your home. But it occurred to me that to be entreated to return by Sir Rowan Heath would prove so mortifying as to render you unwilling to obey the promptings of your natural good sense. Consequently, I donned a disguise. The yeoman who interrupted you and his lordship at the inn was none other than myself. I tell you this now, because I could not do so earlier, knowing how vexing it would prove to learn that you had unburdened your heart to the very man of whom you spoke so tenderly. Perhaps I ought to have revealed my identity then and there, but I wished only to spare you distress. Before you confided your true feelings to the yeoman, I believed you hated me. But if you did not hate me then, surely you do now, as you read what must give you pain. I send you this by way of farewell. May you be happy all your days.

I am yours, etc.,
R.H.

When she finished reading, Catherine put the writing desk on her lap and wrote a single line in reply:

Dear Sir Rowan,
I would be much obliged to you if you would meet me at the pond.

Yours,
C.N.

SHE WAS STANDING at the edge of the pond when he approached. The morning had broken sunny and warm, and she wore a straw bonnet with a green ribbon. She watched a pair of swans glide over the water, then turned when she heard Sir Rowan come up. Gravely, he drew near. Briefly, they exchanged a glance. Silently, she handed him the paper she held in her hand.

He looked at the paper. "It is a poem," he said.

"If you will notice, its subject is the swan, that oddly faithful creature you used to speak of."

He set his jaw grimly. "So it is," he said.

"As it is about a swan, I thought you would be the proper person to consult."

With an effort, he took his eyes from her and read the poem. "This is only superficially about a swan," he said at last. "This is a love sonnet, and I decline to review it."

"You need not review it. Only tell me if I have accurately described the swan."

Although his voice was low, it was passionate as he said, "I cannot read this and fix my mind on its accuracy of description. I cannot stand here and pretend I am the careless fellow who once reviewed a book of yours. Perhaps if I were that man I would be able to feel less and say more."

Catherine took heart from his speech. "Do you mean, sir, that if that swan who is sunning himself over there should rush at me so threateningly that I was seized with a sudden fainting fit, you would still be willing to catch me in your arms?"

After a pause, he replied, "Yes, I should catch you in my arms. I should even do my best to not drop you."

"I thank you for being so open with me. Such candour deserves a similar openness on my part. I must tell you that I knew all along you were the yeoman."

His eyes narrowed as he studied her. "Then you knew you were confiding in me all the time."

"I'm afraid I did. I'm afraid I flattered myself that once you heard what my feelings were, you would declare your undying love for me and we would live happily ever after, like Orsino and Viola."

Stepping near to her he asked, "How did you know who I was?"

"I received the first hint of it in your reference to a swan. Familiar pieces of costume confirmed my suspicion."

He smiled. "Ah, then it was not my performance that gave me away. Surely you have never seen such a tender-hearted, loving old father, grieving for his ungrateful runaway child."

She returned his smile. "Are you asking my opinion of your performance? Very well, then, you shall have it:

Sir Rowan Heath's recent portrayal of an aged yeoman on the stage of the Blue Bottle Theatre was a triumph of sensibility. As the raging father, the illustrious baronet, known principally for his witty political essays and vile poetical reviews, fairly equalled Kemble in nuance of expression. His earlier listless rendition of Duke Orsino is redeemed by this devoted, paternal yeoman speaking in a rural accent of unknown derivation. Yet despite the gentleman's superlative performance, this reviewer is compelled to advise him to give over acting and take up the career of husband, for which he is eminently suited."

Methodically, he wound her bonnet strings about his

hands and pulled them so that her lips came within an inch of his. "Before I consent to the marryin' of ye," he said, assuming the yeoman's gruff voice, "ye must tell me ye won't be stoppin' at any inns with such a blagguard as that Byron fellow."

"I promise to pass all my nights at inns with you. No doubt you will be as enthralled with my new sonnets as his lordship was."

Resuming his own voice, he said, "I confess I would have my mind on matters other than your sonnets, my love. As to your earlier suggestion, I shall agree to accept the role of husband, if you will promise to play opposite me."

She closed her eyes as he kissed them. "I can't tell you how relieved I am to hear you say that. I was afraid you would try to substitute Miss Perrot for me again."

He laughed as he kissed her lightly on the forehead. "Catherine, as the yeoman, I could not tell you what my feelings were. But now, I do take the liberty of declaring my undying love for you. I adore you, and have since that first night we drank Perrot's port."

"And you promise we will live happily ever after, just like Orsino and Viola?"

"If the poor clown had not been banished from our play, I should quote you his best line, 'Trip no further pretty sweeting: Journeys end in lovers meeting, every wise man's son doth know.' But as we have pencilled out these noble sentiments, I shall be reduced to kissing you instead."

"Rowan, I love you very much."

He held her to him urgently. "Catherine, you are not afraid of me?"

"No."

"Suppose I were to kiss you—I mean *really* kiss you? You would not treat me to a review afterward, I hope?"

She gazed at him. "Are you going to kiss me—I mean *really* kiss me?"

He did not keep her any longer in suspense. Immediately he pressed his mouth to hers, and if there was anything to criticize in the length, the manner, or the execution of the kiss, they were content to spend a lifetime discovering it.